RAILROAD
to the MOON

❧ *Elijah's Story* ❧

Jean Flahive (signature)

Jean M. Flahive

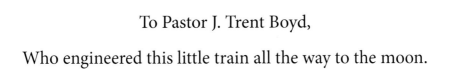

To Pastor J. Trent Boyd,

Who engineered this little train all the way to the moon.

To the reader:

Dialogue that is in italics reflects actual statements of the individuals speaking.

ACKNOWLEDGMENTS

Foreword

For over three years I stalled writing *Railroad to the Moon*. I stalled because I needed to create an authentic voice for one of Maine's forgotten heroes, Oren Cheney, a Freewill Baptist, who was to be a major character in my story. Ironically, my foot dragging came to an end with Kelsey Harrington, a high school senior at the time who was "job-shadowing" me as part of her career exploration project. During the project period, I exposed Kelsey to a full range of writer activities. At its conclusion, Kelsey reminded me that I had not followed through on one promised activity: an interview with a professional, which in this case was a Baptist minister. I had hoped she wouldn't remember.

I frantically renewed my on-again-off-again search, settling on a "cold call" with the pastor of the Freewill Baptist Church in Buxton, Maine—in large part because the church still carried its historic name, Freewill. I reached Pastor Trent Boyd, and shortly thereafter, Kelsey and I met with him.

Call it a miracle or divine intervention, but in our interview with Pastor Boyd, I knew immediately that I had found Oren Cheney's voice. With a passion for history, Pastor Boyd delved into the life of Oren Cheney and became as excited as I was to shed light on this remarkable man. Pastor Boyd's energy and enthusiasm, and his incredible skill at finding the impossible, pulled my little "train" out of the station at last. We were on our way to the moon. Pastor Boyd played a large part in creating this story, and I am forever grateful to him.

I am deeply grateful to Amy Canfield, who edited my first novel, *Billy Boy, The Sunday Soldier of the 17th Maine*. She's up there with the best, and even when I thought this train was rolling along, she pulled me off the track a few times and headed me in a better direction. Her sage advice made all the difference.

I also want to thank William Hierstein, who unknowingly sparked the idea for this story; Elaine Ardia, archives supervisor at the Muskie Archives & Special Collections Library, Bates College, Lewiston, Maine, for her kindness and research support; Gladys Stuart Miller for her history of Lebanon Academy; Nancy Heiser, for long believing in me and always finding ways to improve my storytelling; and Faith DeAngelis for teaching me about bear scat!

A special thank you to my sister, Joanna Italia, for looking over my shoulder and correcting my grammar as she has since childhood. In spite of my sister's excellent command of grammar, I also passed the manuscript on to my writer friend, Ann Leigh. And for her keen insight, I am grateful.

Thank you to Kerry Moody LaPointe for the book's beautiful cover. Kerry's art work is incredible, and I will cherish it forever.

Thank you to the former students of Noble High School in Berwick, Maine, who over the years asked me to tell Elijah's story. It inspired me to write this book.

And always, to my husband, Bill, who owns my heart.

"If you hear the dogs, keep going. If you see the torches in the woods, keep going.
If there's shouting after you, keep going. Don't ever stop. Keep going. If you want a taste of freedom, keep going."
—Harriet Tubman, African American abolitionist

PROLOGUE
September 1863

The bloodhounds were close, their hoarse-ringing bays shattering the silent stillness of the forest. They would overtake him soon. He shot a glance in either direction and ran deeper into the woods, toward the nearby ridge. Branches lashed his face and arms. He stumbled, catching a bare foot on a protruding tree root. He fell hard onto the ground, but fear drove him to his feet. He fled down the steep embankment, weaving his way through its jagged outcroppings. When he reached the bottom, his eyes panned the narrow ravine for a place to hide. Then he spotted the hounds running along the ridge. They found his trail down the rocky embankment. A rifle shot cracked the air, its bullet splintering into a tree only inches from his head. No time to hide. He scrambled up the ledge to the other side.

Sweat trickled down his back and he winced in pain, his wounds from the last whipping splitting open in the unrelenting chase. Water—he must find water to conceal his scent and throw off the bloodhounds.

He reached the top of the ridge, gasping, inhaling huge gulps of air. A deer spooked in front of him and disappeared in a narrow opening through dense thicket. He followed the small doe, hoping the deer path would lead him to her watering hole. But the path opened onto a clearing, leaving him exposed to the slave catchers and the dogs. Frantic, he ran along the clearing's edge, eager for the cover of the woods.

Bear scat.

He leaned over and touched it. Warm.

The bloodhounds bayed behind him. They had reached his side of the ravine, and soon would break through the woods. Too close.

He pushed his bare feet into the bear scat and, using his hands, smeared it up and down his legs. He ran into the copse of trees and then stopped, fearful the hounds would hear him crashing through the woods. He hid behind a thick oak, hoping the scat would disguise his scent. The hounds entered the clearing, massive, powerful beasts with long heads and wrinkled skin. Two slave catchers came into view. Then a third man emerged from the thicket, his broad chest heaving, his shirt soaked with sweat. Buckra! No! The brutal overseer who had lashed him repeatedly since he first arrived at the Fowler plantation.

The bloodhounds reached the scat. Their black noses feverishly sniffed at the ground.

Shouts.

"It's scat! They're sniffing the dang bear scat!"

"Confound it! Git 'em moving!"

The handler urged his dogs forward. But they continued to circle the scat, noses to the ground.

"Why them hounds circling this here scat?"

The handler glanced down. The bear scat had been disturbed. "Your runaway stepped in it is why. Thought he might lose the dogs. Confused 'em for a moment, but they've picked up his scent again."

The hounds raced across the meadow.

Stories of runaways torn to pieces by bloodhounds unleashed his adrenaline. Panicked, he ran wildly, his arms and legs snagging branches, the dried limbs snapping noisily like shots from a rifle.

The dogs breached the forest. It was over.

Terror welled in his throat. He dropped to the forest floor, curled into a ball, using his arms to protect his face.

Howling, the hounds circled him.

Then a voice, familiar, frightening. He opened his eyes. It was him. Buckra.

A horrifying grin wormed across the overseer's face. "Bet you was thinking them hound dogs gonna tear you to pieces."

A long, sharp blade flickered in Buckra's outstretched hand. "That's for me to do."

"No, suh! No! No!"

His body shook; his arms flailed the air.

"Elijah! Elijah, it's me, Jamie. Wake up! It's only a nightmare."

"When peoples care for you and cry for you,
they can straighten out your soul."
Langston Hughes, grandson of Charles Langston, former slave

CHAPTER 1
October 1863

"This here's arithmetic," said Jamie, balancing a handful of bruised apples along a fence rail.

"No, suh, them only apples on the fence," Elijah said with a shake of his head.

"Needing them apples to show you how to use numbers." Jamie lined the apples in single file. "See, this here's six apples," and pointing his finger, he counted each one, "one, two, three—." When he finished, he picked up four apples and stuffed them into the wide pocket of his overalls. "Now how many apples is left on the fence?"

"Why you go and take them apples and put them in your pocket?"

"That's arithmetic. I just went and subtracted them, is all."

"Jamie, suh go and eats them apples all by hisself?" Elijah frowned.

"I ain't eating them apples!"

"Elijah share his apples. That just the way it be."

"It ain't about sharing," Jamie said in a defeated tone. "It's about arithmetic. Guess I ain't teaching so good."

Elijah scanned the ground. Then he leaned over and picked up a handful of apples. Placing four on the fence, he said, "Now Elijah got six apples. Two more than Jamie, suh got in his pocket. Jamie, suh teach Elijah this arithmetic good," he said with a wink, ruffling the boy's hair.

Jamie tried to hide his grin. "Thing is, reading's going to be a lot harder. I'll be learning you soon enough. You want to play checkers?"

"Elijah go to the meadow now."

Ten-year-old Jamie nodded. Although Elijah had been with his family for nearly three months and was growing more comfortable with them by the day, he often wandered alone, haunted still by his years as a slave, struggling to find purchase with freedom and a new family.

"You thinking about your nightmare?"

"Elijah work it out after a time."

"Want me to walk with you?"

Elijah smiled and shook his head no. "You go on and set them checkers on the board. Be in soon enough."

"All right, then."

Leaning his elbows on the fence post, Elijah gazed out across the meadow, the stand of oak and maple trees at its edge, the brilliance of their autumn leaves fading against the dying light. It was too early to see the stars, but Elijah imagined they were there, patiently waiting to make their appearance. He would always hold close to his heart the North Star, his miracle star that had led him out of slavery and to freedom. While the Civil War raged in his distant homeland, he now wandered peacefully on a small farm in Maine, the Laird farm. Billy's home. How sorely he missed his friend, the first white folk who had been nice to him. But Billy was gone—shot by a firing squad for deserting the Union Army and going home. Billy had been called a simpleton, lacking in common intelligence, and for this reason, pleas had been made to spare his life. Mister Laird had told Elijah that a pardon from President Lincoln had been issued for his son but that it did not arrive in time. Billy was executed at Fort Preble, inside the ramparts overlooking Portland Harbor.

Images of Billy flashed through his mind—their perilous wade in the Potomac River so close to where Billy had been bivouacked with the 17th Maine, racing across open fields, stumbling in utter darkness, all to elude the slave catchers and the army. He shuddered as he remembered their near capture in a Maryland barn and their harrowing escape from the train station in Philadelphia. Anna Dickinson's gentle face and cinnamon eyes materialized in front of him. Anna, the young Quaker who had risked her own life to save his and Billy's. The last time he saw Billy was in Philadelphia before he was guided out of the city on the Underground Railroad, the large network of secret routes and safe houses used by runaway slaves to escape to Canada. Fearful of being captured and shot for desertion, Billy had exacted a promise from Elijah before they separated—to come to Maine the following summer and, if need be, watch over his younger brother Jamie. To take his place.

After he arrived in Canada, Elijah had lived in a boarding house in a small town not far from the border with Vermont. He worked as part of a logging crew deep in the primal forests, harvesting pine and fir for the burgeoning sawmills, spending weeks at a time in primitive logging camps. Although grateful for his small wage, he had hated the desolate cold, the timbering, when all he had ever known was farming. During his weeks in the forests, most of the white loggers spoke a language he didn't understand—French, he was told by the missus who owned the boarding house. And although he lived and worked with other runaway slaves, he had kept mostly to himself, toiling tirelessly, unable to chase away the demons of his past, and in his quiet despair, he felt a yawning loneliness.

He remembered experiencing his first northern winter, watching ice form around the edges of a lake, slowly transforming the vast body of water into a hard, nearly impenetrable freeze. A fisherman had explained to him that beneath the ice the water teemed with life, dormant to man, until the spring thaws. Elijah likened it to the deepest reaches of his heart, where his pappy still lived, dormant, waiting for his return, if such a spring were possible. As the stinging winter winds enveloped him, Elijah looked to the following summer, his wanting to see Billy the only warmth that penetrated his disquieted soul. In early August, determined to keep his promise, he had set out on foot, crossing the border into Vermont and on to New Hampshire, following the Saco River to the sea, and finally reaching Berwick, Maine. Yet after two weeks of making his way, he learned he had arrived a month too late; his friend Billy was already cold in his grave.

Elijah tapped a fisted hand against his heart. "Right here, Billy, suh, you livin' right here."

He pushed open the fence gate and walked through the meadow in silence, recalling his unexpected arrival at the Laird farm. Jamie had spotted him walking up the lane and immediately had run away from him. Elijah had worried the child might be fearful of a colored man, for although he was of medium height and only sixteen, he knew he struck an imposing figure with his broad shoulders and muscular arms. And after Jamie's timidity, he had to summon his will to walk up the porch steps. But Mr. Laird had greeted him warmly, and then, with great sadness, had shared with him the news of Billy's execution. Jamie, he said, had retreated into a private, voiceless world since his brother's death. The doctor believed that Jamie was grieving in his own way, and would speak in his own time. Mr. Laird had told how each evening since his brother's death, Jamie would set his wooden checkerboard on the floor, put each red and black checker in place, and then rock back and forth, staring vacantly at the painted squares, waiting for a turn that never came.

Later that same day Elijah had visited Billy's grave, unaware that the boy had stealthily followed him through the woods. Hearing a twig snap behind him, he had turned to find the sad-faced child intently studying him. Blue eyes met brown. Desperate to learn anything Elijah could tell him about his brother, Jamie's self-imposed exile came to an end.

Shy and awkward with one another, each had tested his boundaries; Jamie poised to defend his brother from any perceived affront, but none came. Emotionally spent, Jamie had collapsed on the ground and began rocking, his head folded in his arms. Elijah remembered dropping to the forest floor and pulling Jamie close to him, holding the child as one would hold a small bird that had fallen from its nest. As Jamie rocked, he rocked with him, telling how Billy had once held him in the same way when he found Elijah close to dying on the banks of Goose Creek. "You go and cry, Jamie, suh, 'til all them tears fall out."

He didn't remember how long he held him, but the child at last lifted his face and, wiping the wetness from his eyes, asked Elijah if he could learn him checkers. Elijah quietly thanked a merciful God. "Elijah go and take care of him good, just like Billy, suh want. Yes, suh, Elijah keep this promise, no matter," he said out loud as he stared at the starlit sky.

Elijah had been overwhelmed by the kindheartedness of Billy's folks, but his easy affection for Jamie caught him by surprise. Jamie was the mirror of Billy—wiry body, sandy blond hair, and ever-so-gentle blue eyes. He was a smart child, and although he had been aware of his brother's limitations, he had also worshipped him. In his unrelenting grief, he chose Elijah to fill the empty hole left by Billy's death.

When Elijah reluctantly made preparations to return to Canada, the Lairds had asked him if would like to stay on. He had readily accepted.

Now, as night settled across the meadows, Elijah turned and glanced at the farmhouse. The glow of a lantern's light swayed back and forth, followed by Jamie's muffled call. "You're needing to come in, Elijah. Figure it's time for checkers."

"Elijah on his way, Jamie, suh."

*"The distant soul can shake the distant friend's soul
and make the longing felt, over untold miles."*
John Masefield

CHAPTER 2
April 1865

Elijah welcomed the sights and smells of the warming spring, the thawing earth yielding pleasantly beneath his feet. The last vestiges of hard-packed snow, mottled grayish-brown, melted in the shadowed places of the surrounding barnyard. A year and a half with the Lairds had come and gone, leaving him at last with a blessed feeling that he was now a part of their family. He whistled as he entered the barn. Daisy, the old mare, raised her head as if responding to his call.

"Just cleaning your stall, Daisy." He led the horse outside and as he tied her to a post, she nudged her cold nostrils against his overall pockets. "Ain't got nuthin' for you this time, girl," he said, nudging her head gently to the side. He resumed his whistling, pushed the wheelbarrow into the barn, and, with his pitchfork, stabbed at the dirtied straw.

"Elijah, come quick!" Jamie rushed into the barn, his cheeks ruddy with color. "I think Mother Pig's giving birth and Pa ain't here!"

Oblivious to the muddied ground, both dropped to their knees and huddled close to Mother Pig as she grunted her discomfort.

"Jamie, suh, fetch some clean straw. It keep them little ones warm."

Moments later, the first greased suckling appeared headfirst. Several minutes passed, and following a squeal from Mother Pig, another suckling popped out and onto the straw. Over the next three hours, the process repeated itself several more times. Elijah carefully examined each tiny suckling like a practiced midwife before he handed it to Jamie, who tucked it with the others against the mother's warm belly.

When the afterbirth at last discharged, Elijah and Jamie, flushed with nervous exhaustion, rested their backs against the fence.

"We got us ten healthy-looking piglets," said Jamie. He watched as Mother Pig's eyes fluttered and closed. "She's plum wore out."

"She be fine." Elijah reached over and stroked Mother Pig's head. "This make Elijah remember."

"When you were a slave?"

Elijah shook his head. "No, with Billy, suh. We was hiding by the creek, and he tell me when he in the army his friend Leighton go and buy this big old sow from a farmer."

"Why'd he do that?"

"Keep her 'til they ain't got no food to eat. But right off this sow go and have ten piglets, same as Mother Pig."

Jamie sat up on his haunches. "What'd they do?"

Elijah began to laugh. "Billy, suh, all he worry about is to give them piglets names."

"Yeah, that's Billy all right."

"Said them soldiers poked fun, but he say them pigs is got to have names."

"So did they name them?"

"Yes, suh. They was named after them army forts along the Potomac."

"Then let's do ours the same."

"What them forts called, Jamie, suh?"

Mother Pig squealed in her sleep, shifted her body.

Jamie shrugged his shoulders. "Don't know. Maybe Pa does. When he comes home I'll ask him."

"They didn't get to keep them piglets. Army was moving out next day. Billy, suh say his friend have to go and give the sow and them piglets back to the farmer."

Jamie scrunched his nose. "Bad luck. We'll give our piglets different names."

They sat awhile longer in silence, content to watch the piglets squirm and suckle.

"Elijah? Why'd the army need twelve men to shoot Billy?"

Elijah tried to hold back his surprise at the out-of-the-blue question. It had been nearly two years since Billy's death, and in all that time, Jamie had never asked him about the execution. Elijah took a deep breath.

"You sure you want to talk about this, Jamie, suh?"

"Sometimes I think on it. Why'd it take so many soldiers to kill him?"

"And you ain't never asked your pa?"

"Naw. He still don't feel right about letting Billy muster. Don't want to make him feel bad by asking."

A tiny squeal erupted from the straw as a piglet fell from the litter and landed on its back. Elijah recognized the runt; it was having difficulty fighting for its mother's milk. Gently he tucked the smallest piglet into the middle of the litter and waited until its mouth found Mother Pig's teat.

"Remember that time Reverend Snow come and meet Elijah?" Without waiting for an answer, Elijah continued. "He tell me about Billy and what they done. Elijah ask him same question."

"You did? What'd he say?"

"He say army have all them soldiers there so if one or two don't fire his rifle, or they go and miss, they still enough shots to make sure Billy dead. He say if they have all them many firing, no one know if he go and make the killing shot. Army also don't put gunpowder in one of them twelve bullets. Soldiers don't know who gots that one."

"Why does the army do that?"

"Soldiers don't like shooting their own folk. They hope maybe they not the one who done the killing."

"I heard Pa tell Mr. Ricker that Billy, he got five bullets right to his heart." Jamie looked down at the ground.

Placing his arm around the boy's shoulders, Elijah said, "Jamie, suh, what we fixin' to do with all them piglets?"

"For sure I ain't giving them away, like Billy and Leighton done." Elijah laughed.

Jamie leaned into Elijah's shoulder. Using the sleeve of his shirt, he wiped a single tear from his face. "I ain't never giving you away, neither."

Shadows had lengthened across the farmyard by the time Elijah and Jamie left the pigpen, satisfied that all was well with Mother Pig. Elijah led Daisy back into the barn and her partially cleaned stall. It was late; he would finish mucking it out in the morning. The horse whinnied in pleasure when he reached for a bucket and poured oats into her empty trough.

Boots stomped across the timbered floor, John Laird's long, heavy stride at once familiar. He was a tall man, and in spite of his slender build, his bearing suggested strength and his firm jaw and deep-set eyes matched his rugged and handsome face.

"Mistah John." Elijah backed out of the horse's stall, the bucket and pitchfork in his hands.

"Got news for you, son."

"For me, Mistah John?" Elijah stopped, set down the bucket, and crossed his hands over the pitchfork's handle. "What that be?"

"It's all good, Elijah. Folks in town say the war's coming to an end. City of Richmond, the capitol of the Confederacy, fell to the Union forces. General Lee's expected to surrender in the next few days." He pulled his pipe from his pocket, took a long, hesitating look, and tucked it away. "Your people are free."

Elijah stood in stunned silence.

"I'll leave you be with your thoughts. I'm sure there'll be more news any day now." John turned as if to leave, then stopped and looked back at Elijah. "Oh, and son, being in town made me realize you ain't been there in a long time. I'm going back to Blaisdell's Store in a few days to pick up the supplies I ordered. I'd like you to come with me."

Elijah shuddered. In finding solace with the Lairds, he purposely had chosen to limit his world to the occasional guests at the farm, reveling in the comfort and security of his small family. Even Jamie's teacher, Mary Rogers, had asked him if he would like to attend the public school, but he had shyly declined. In the end, Jamie had taken upon himself the role of tutor, and while his ability to instruct was limited, Elijah was learning to read.

"Elijah stay here, Mistah John."

"You think on that, too. It's long past time. You've as much right to walk in the street as any man." John disappeared from the barn.

Elijah found himself shaking. He grasped the barn's center beam to steady himself. Freedom. What would it all mean for him? And for Pappy, so far away at Mastuh Ramsey's farm? A sudden ache winnowed across his chest; his heart throbbed against his ribs. What was it the Canadian fisherman had said? "Even though you can't see it, life teems beneath the frozen lake, waiting for spring." Was freedom to be his spring? Pappy a part of his life again? Pappy had been an older man when he married his mama, and now Elijah asked himself, was Pappy even alive? Were any of the others he knew still there? He thought of Talitha, his sweet childhood friend, the girl he had once kissed in a cornfield. He wondered if she even remembered him, or perhaps had even been sold, lost to him forever. He completed the last of his chores at a feverish pace. So many questions raced through his mind. And he had no answer for any of them.

"The soul that is within me no man can degrade."
Frederick Douglass, African American abolitionist, social reformer

CHAPTER 3

Blaisdell's Store sat squarely on the corner of Milk and Berwick streets, the busiest corner in the burgeoning mill town along the Salmon Falls River. John pulled the wagon to a stop, climbed down from the buckboard, and tied Daisy to the post, appeasing her with a thick carrot he had taken from his cold cellar. He looked up at Elijah still sitting on the seat. "You coming in?"

"Maybe Elijah stay."

"I'd like you to see some folks, friends of mine."

With a heavy sigh Elijah nodded. "Elijah be in soon." His eyes followed John into the store. He took a deep breath and glanced up and down the dusty street of Berwick, a town he lived in but barely knew. Perhaps Mistah John had been right. It was time to step out of the shelter of the farm. Across the Salmon Falls River he heard the train whistle its departure from Somersworth, the mills on the banks clanging noisily as river water turned the wheels and belts of the mills' machineries. White folk scurrying by glanced his way, their faces expressing something between surprise and curiosity. Alone on the buckboard, he began to feel as if he sat high on a perch like an anxious sparrow. A plump, pretty woman with flaxen hair brushed past the wagon, an empty basket flapping in her hand. Before entering the store, she turned to him, smiled, and said hello. He shot back a nervous grin. Her gesture soothed him, but only briefly.

Two men emerged from the alley and, spotting him on the buckboard, stopped in their tracks and stared.

Elijah stiffened. Suddenly he wanted off the wagon, off his

uncomfortable perch.

Slowly, hands in their pockets, the two men swaggered toward him like cocky roosters crossing the barnyard.

"Say now, Weldon, I reckon this here's the darkie been taking Billy's place."

"Yes, sir, Lewis, I'm thinking you may right." Spittle flew at the spokes of a wagon's wheel.

"Billy," said Lewis with a smirk. "Dumber than a box of rocks." Laughing at his own joke, he paused and then said, "We used to enjoy watching Billy squirm. He'd run off like a frightened cub looking for his ma."

"I'm thinking, Lewis, this darkie's done his share of squirming, being a slave and all. I'd like to have seen that."

"Maybe we will soon enough, Weldon, maybe we will."

More laughter.

Enough. Elijah stood, met their eyes. He was used to ridicule, forced to take it from Buckra, unable to strike back, but it both angered and saddened him to hear the taunts about Billy. No more.

He jumped off the wagon. As much as he wanted to distance himself from the two white men and his own increasing rage, he stood firm, placed his hands on his hips, striking an imposing presence.

The two men stopped laughing. Fear reddened their faces.

Although his feet moved forward at a normal pace, Elijah's blood quickened with each step, closing the space between them.

The two men stepped back, out of his way. Let him pass.

Elijah hurried up the wooden platform that fronted the store, relief washing over him as he disappeared through the door.

The aroma of coffee and spice assailed his nostrils. He scanned the aisles looking for Mistah John, spotted him standing around a potbellied stove with a small group of men.

"My gracious, Elijah!"

He turned to see a pleasant looking woman behind the counter, her graying hair pulled back from her rosy-cheeked face. "You might not remember me, it's been so long. I'm Harriet Blaisdell, the proprietor's wife."

Elijah offered a small smile. "Ma'am." His breathing slowed. "Elijah remember."

"Elijah, some folks here I want you to meet." John beckoned him with a wave of his arm.

"This is Freddie Biggs," John said, turning his face to the man beside him, and this is Tom Piper and Clay Ricker."

Saying nothing, Elijah nodded to each.

"Good to meet you, Elijah. Been friends with the Lairds all my life," said Tom. "You couldn't have a nicer family to be with as far as I'm concerned."

"Yes, suh."

"Elijah," said Freddie. "It's in the papers this morning. Lee surrendered at Appomattox. The long war is over."

For the next half hour Elijah listened as the men talked around the stove about the aftermath of the war, the local boys they hoped would soon be coming home. Occasionally he nodded and when called upon, he offered a short, friendly response, but mostly he stood silently while the men nattered, argued, and laughed. His spirits bounded when John at last gathered his supplies and said it was time to head for home.

On his way out, Harriett handed him a small bag of licorice strings. "Have some if you'd like, Elijah, but I know for sure they're Jamie's favorite."

Throughout the remainder of the day, Elijah worked in the fields, and as the sun slipped behind the tall pines that loomed beyond the stone wall, he drove the small milking herd into the barn, knowing Mistah John would be waiting. It felt good to be home, alone with his chores. More and more he became aware of his inherent shyness. And as fine a people as the Lairds were, he had sometimes asked himself if he would have stayed had it not been for Jamie. What had begun as a promise to Billy had become an unshakeable bond with a young boy.

As was their custom, Elijah and John worked mostly in silence milking the cows, and when they were halfway through, John said, "I'll finish up here. Reckon Jamie's ready for your schooling."

Elijah wiped the day's dried sweat from his forehead, cleaned the dirt and straw from his boots, and headed for the house.

Stepping into the mudroom off the kitchen, he slipped off his wet boots, setting them neatly beside the door. He hung his jacket on the wall peg and in his stocking feet entered the warmth of the kitchen. Jamie sat at the table, his schoolbooks spread across its top.

"We'll be reading *Walden*, by Henry David Thoreau," Jamie said without looking up.

Elijah washed his hands at the sink's pump and then pulled a chair to the table. He frowned at the book's many pages.

"What this *Walden* about, no how?"

"This fella Thoreau left the city to go and live in the woods near a pond, Walden Pond, for two years. All by himself."

"Why he do that? He colored? He hidin' from slave catchers?"

"Naw, he ain't colored. Miss Rogers says we got to read the first two chapters. Then we're needin' to tell her why this here Thoreau went and cut out to the woods."

"You go and read. Elijah tired. This all too many pages."

Jamie read out loud, struggling with the many difficult words. By the end of the first two chapters, he crinkled his nose. "Don't know that I'd run off to the woods when I got me all them nice things in the city. Why you think he cut out like that?"

"Jamie, suh, he don't be needing them city things. Like when Elijah work in the fields. Nighttime come, moon over our heads, coloreds all sit by the fire. Sometimes we just sing. Ain't no need for other things." Elijah took a deep breath. "'Cept freedom."

"Pa says you're really free now."

Elijah nodded. "Elijah know when you gots freedom, you don't need nuthin' more. Mmm-hmm. Life be simple, like the man say."

"You thinkin' that's what I tell my teacher?"

"Yes, suh. Ain't no need for all them fancy words tell us so."

Late in the evening as Elijah sat alone in the kitchen, the clatter of approaching hooves shattered his quiet musings. Who would be arriving at the Laird farm well after dark? In spite of the war's near end, the image of slave catchers prowling the countryside to reclaim their bounties remained for him an ever-present fear.

"Mistah John," he said, rushing into the sitting room. "Horse be coming up the way. Ain't nobody come this late afore."

"Most likely a neighbor in need, is all," said John, his voice calm. Still, he grabbed the lantern off the table, the wide floorboards creaking under his hurried stride. A horse whinnied. He stepped out onto the porch, closing the door behind him.

Elijah waited in anxious silence.
Boots scuffled across the porch.
The hairs on the back of Elijah's neck pricked.
The door cracked open.
"Elijah! Fetch Jamie and the missus!"

"The most successful war seldom pays for its losses."
—Thomas Jefferson

CHAPTER 4

Harry Warren stood in the middle of the sitting room. His tousled hair, darkened by sweat, lay matted across his forehead; a wide smile filled his handsome, chiseled face. Letting out a huge yelp, Jamie ran across the floor.

"What a sight for sore eyes you are," said Martha Laird. "Three long years since you been gone, but don't you look just grand." She wrapped her arms around him and pulled him close. "Thank the good Lord you're home."

Tilting back his head, Harry thought the years had been kind to Billy's mother. Her wavy brown hair, coiled in a long braid, fell halfway down her back, and even though fine lines creased her brow, her gray-blue eyes commanded her face. "You're pretty as ever, Miss Martha." He swallowed hard. "I'm so sorry about Billy. I did what I could for him. There wasn't a day that I didn't wonder what happened to him, worried for him—"

"Hush now," she interrupted. "If he hadn't been transferred to another unit, I believe he would've been just fine with you at his side."

"Tell me about the fighting, Harry," pleaded Jamie, tugging on the sleeve of his jacket. "Did you bring your musket?"

"In time, my young friend, in time. Besides, didn't you used to say I was too big for my britches?"

"Aw, Harry, I was just a kid then."

"Elijah," said John. "This is Harry Warren, Billy's good friend. Used to watch out for my son. Seems the older Billy got, the bullying only became worse. Then Harry stepped in. Put an end to it."

Elijah recalled the two men from town who had taunted him. In his mind's eye, he saw Harry standing up to them, pushing back, Billy at his side. He looked at Harry and felt an instant kinship.

"Elijah." Harry's voice cracked with emotion. Extending his hand, he said, "My Mary wrote me about you. Someday, I want to hear every word, hear every moment you spent with Billy."

"Yes, suh." Elijah firmly accepted Harry's hand. "And Billy, suh, he talk about you."

"He was right special to me." Harry turned and looked at John. "I'm proud to have served, Mister John, but it ain't right what they done to Billy. Lots of folks called it a travesty of justice."

"At least President Lincoln saw fit to pardon him. Billy never belonged in the army in the first place, and I have to live with my decision to let him muster."

"Elijah's been a real blessing to us," said Martha.

"He's my big brother now," said Jamie. "It's what Billy wanted."

"How'd you make it home this early?" John asked, at once eager to change the subject. "Thinking it would be weeks before our boys showed up in town."

"Got wounded at Hatcher's Run during the siege of Petersburg. Thought I might lose my leg there for a while. I was in the hospital tent for a time. Leg's healed pretty good, 'cept now I got a bit of a limp. Captain said the war was coming to an end soon enough, and sent me home."

"Well, reckon it's time to be a farmer now. That piece of land of yours is just waiting to be cleared."

"Yes, sir, but I've got some unfinished business first."

"Whatever is that?" Martha asked.

"Leighton." Harry turned his face to Elijah. "He was our friend, too. Billy, Leighton, Charlie, Josh, and me, we all mustered together. Then Leighton was shot. Only four months into the war."

"So he dead?" Elijah suddenly turned and looked at Jamie. "Elijah remember this name. Leighton be the one who buy that sow and got them piglets."

Harry laughed. "Oh, I remember. That was Leighton all right. He was killed at the Battle of Fredericksburg. Held him in my arms. Before he died he begged me not to leave him there, to bring his big old bones home to Maine, and that's what I'm going to do."

"It would mean everything to his folks," said John, "but I read where thousands were buried in shallow graves on the battlefield. How will you ever find his body?"

"Charlie, Josh, and me buried him during a short truce, so we marked it with some stones. Mostly, I memorized the field, stepped it out using some landmarks. Make no mistake, I'll find him."

Harry paused, bit down on his lower lip. "Something else I'm wantin' to do while I'm down South."

"Josh," said John. "I bet you're going to look for Josh."

Elijah looked confused. "This other friend, he dead, too?"

"Don't know. He's been in one of them prison camps."

"Do you know which one?" Martha asked.

"During the Petersburg Campaign he was captured and taken first to the prison in Danville, Virginia. Captain Merrill found out Josh was among a number of men later transferred to Salisbury prison in North Carolina. If I leave right off, I just might get there when they release all the prisoners, find Josh, and bring him home. And, well, if he didn't make it, then there'll be two bodies I'll be bringing back."

Elijah took an anxious step forward. "Salisbury, suh?"

Harry furrowed his brow. "You know something about Salisbury?"

Elijah felt his whole body shake. "Elijah go with you."

"What do you—?"

"Mistah John!" Elijah turned sharply to him.

"What's wrong, Elijah? Why are you trembling?" John asked.

"Elijah need to go with Harry, suh."

The room went eerily quiet. John paced across the floor, turned and paced back again. "What's this about, Elijah? Why Salisbury?"

Jamie's eyes darted back and forth between his pa and Elijah, his face already pale with worry.

"Pappy live not so far from there. Mastuh take us to town when he sell his crop. Please, Mistah John. You say coloreds be free now. But Elijah ain't never be free in here," he said, pointing a finger at his heart, "'til he find his pappy again."

Harry shook his head. "It's not that I wouldn't welcome the company, but I reckon it's still not entirely safe for coloreds down South."

"Mistah John say the war be over." Elijah looked at John, his eyes pleading.

John blew out his cheeks. "It's going to take time for things to settle down, Elijah. Perhaps when we know it's safer for you to travel—"

"Elijah be with Harry, suh."

"You sure you need to make this trip right off, Harry?" asked John.

"Have to, if I've any chance of finding Josh."

"Please, Mistah John."

John raked his fingers through his hair. "It's not my place to hold you back. But make no mistake, Elijah, this is a great risk you'll be taking."

"No!" Jamie shouted. "No! You promised, Elijah, you promised you'd be my big brother!"

"It only be for a time, Jamie, suh."

"I won't let you go!" He curled his small frame against Elijah's chest.

Wringing her hands in the folds of her apron, Martha said, "Lord, is this family ever going to heal?"

"Hush now, Jamie, suh," Elijah said in low tone. Pulling Jamie's arms away from his waist, he bent down on his knees and placed his hands on the boy's shoulders. "Elijah need to find out about his pappy. Then Elijah come home."

Thin shoulders shook beneath Elijah's wide hands. "But Pa said—"

"Elijah be with Harry, suh. He a soldier. We gone be fine."

"You promise? You promise you'll come home?"

"Got me some schoolin' to finish. Elijah want to know what this Thoreau go and do all the time he in them woods. You read all them words so you can tell Elijah." He saw the hint of a smile tug at edges of Jamie's mouth.

"Elijah come home, Jamie, suh. This my promise."

"To live in hearts we leave behind is not to die."
—Thomas Campbell, *Hallowed Ground*

CHAPTER 5

It was nearly midnight when Elijah raced across the barnyard to the meadow beyond. Flushed and out of breath, he leaned across the rail fence and stared at the myriad stars, his gaze fixed keenly on the southern sky. Pappy.

His mind flooded with memories, harking back to the last time he had seen his father. It was a warm summer morning and he had been heading for the fields when, unexpectedly, Mastuh Ramsey fetched him and led him back to the farmyard. "You've been sold, Elijah. I'm sorry, but you need to get on the wagon. I've gathered your things—the sack is there." Pappy appeared from the barn, rushed to him, his eyes washed in tears. Elijah lingered his goodbye. Suddenly the new mastuh cracked a whip across his shirtless back. Terrified, his back burning with pain, he had climbed despairingly onto the back of the wagon. Leaning into him, Pappy had whispered, "Run my boy, run like the wind." Three horrible months later, Elijah ran.

"Elijah gone find you again, Pappy," he said out loud to the surrounding darkness. A northerly breeze brushed across his face, and he spoke to it. "Maybe this wind carry my words, tell you Elijah coming."

He didn't remember his mama, who died when he was two. Pappy had said she was a fine woman, with silky brown skin and flashing eyes that would set a man's soul on fire. When she caught the fever and lay dying in the cornfield, Pappy had carried her to their hut, to her own plank bed, so that she wouldn't die in the field like some wounded animal. Pappy always said that while he held his Elisha in those last precious moments, she died with grace, as a wife and as a mama to her boy, and not as a slave.

Elijah wondered if Pappy knew he had run away from his new owner, Mastuh Fowler. He was quite certain that Fowler would have taken his anger out against Ramsey, demanding his money back after only three months' time. And if Pappy had heard about his escape, then he may have worried his son was dead. There were too many stories passed on of runaway slaves that did not survive their escape, many killed on the spot when found.

Elijah shivered as much from the night air as from memories of running barefoot through the forest, the howls of the bloodhounds close on his heels. Finally the dogs lost his scent in the blessed cool waters at the bottom of a steep ravine. Weeks passed, and still he ran, his strength depleting, his body starved for nourishment. Finally too weak to go farther, he had collapsed on the banks of Goose Creek, knowing death was at hand. Then Billy found him. Billy had scant food in his haversack, yet he had easily shared it with Elijah, and in doing so, unknowingly saved his life. Fear brought them together, but a crushing need for companionship had forged a fierce bond between them.

In his harrowing run north with Billy, Elijah had crossed the threshold into another world, a world beyond the plantation boundaries that had framed his life. Here, the unexpected kindness from Quakers was abruptly countered by the hatred from the white folk who pursued him and Billy across Maryland and through the streets of Philadelphia. It was all still raw and confusing. In his nightmares, he felt the whip tearing at his back, the stinging pain of each lash, but then a hand, Billy's hand, would reach out and pull him from the dark recesses of his mind. Now the hand that saved him was real, and it was Jamie's.

It was time to push the memories aside. Elijah slowly made his way back to the farmhouse and his room, burying himself in the sanctity of sleep and dreams of finding his father.

*"They shall be safe in their land; and they shall know that I
am the LORD, when I have broken the bands of their yoke and
delivered them from the hand of those who enslaved them."*
—Ezekiel 34:27

CHAPTER 6
April 1865

The train clattered noisily along the rails across the Virginia countryside, wending its way through the rolling hills and into the James River valley, its final destination. Weary from his arduous trip to Washington to seek financial support for his Freewill Baptist college in Maine, Reverend Oren Cheney had made a last-minute decision to take an unscheduled trip to Richmond. He had set forth on the April hiatus between college terms to raise funds, and while in Washington had learned of the fall of Richmond and President Lincoln's visit to the vanquished capital of the Confederacy. The momentous events unfolding such a short distance away had stirred Oren deeply, and with his business in Washington completed, he had hastened to Richmond.

The president had taken his young son Tad with him, and with only an escort of ten sailors, Lincoln had walked the streets of Richmond. Oren picked up the newspaper he had placed on the empty seat beside him and glanced at the article on Lincoln's historic visit, and how emancipated slaves had surrounded the president, many touching him to see if he was real.

"Glory to God!"

"The great Messiah! He's freed his children."

Leaning his head against the seat, Oren hungrily read once again how Lincoln had responded to the jubilant freedmen. *"My poor friends, you are free—free as the air. You can cast off the name of slave and trample upon it; it will come to you no more. Liberty is your birthright. God gave it to you as he gave it to others, and it is a sin that you have been deprived of it for so many years. But you must try to deserve this priceless boon. Let the world see that you merit it, and are able to maintain it by your good works. Don't let your joy carry you into excesses. Learn the laws and obey them; obey God's commandments and thank him for giving you liberty, for him you owe all things. There, now, let me pass on; I have but little time to spare."*

The train lurched unexpectedly, and lowering the newspaper to his lap, Oren glanced out the window, gasping at the skeletal silhouette of Richmond, dark and smoldering in the near distance. In that instance he felt God's duty to celebrate with the victorious that at long last there would be equality for all, but also to reach out to the defeated. President Lincoln had done right, just as Oren's mother, Abigail, had instilled in him those many years ago, *to do right.* Since he was a young man he had spoken out against slavery, using the pulpit and *The Morning Star,* the Freewill Baptist newspaper in Dover, New Hampshire, to expound his fierce abolitionist stand.

"For the defeated, there must be hope," he whispered to himself. "I will begin the healing here, in Richmond, doing God's work." In such defining moments, he often recalled Luther, one of the many runaway slaves escaping to Canada who had been sheltered in his father's home, a station on the Underground Railroad in Peterborough, New Hampshire. Luther arrived at their door in 1828 and twelve-year-old Oren, alone at the time, led the frightened runaway into the cellar. Later, in the sanctity of his hiding place, comforted by a woolen blanket and warmed soup, Luther had asked the boy his name. The slave told him that in the Old Testament the word Oren meant "tree." Then he had placed his bony hand on Oren's head, and prayed. "Let the boy be blessed like the tree he named for, planted by the rivers of water. Lord, don't let his leaves wither, and make whatever this boy do prosperous."

At forty-nine, Oren, a distinguished-looking man with gentility of manner and bearing befitting a scholar, sighed deeply at the still-powerful memory. "Luther, in all these many years I have not forgotten you."

The train pulled to a stop. "Richmond station!" shouted the conductor.

Oren stood and gathered his bags, a prayer in his heart. "Let my work be prosperous."

"Yet, we should mark it—the soldier's grave,
Some one may seek him in hope to save!
Some of the dear ones, far away,
Would bear him home to his native clay:
Twere sad, indeed, should they wander nigh,
Find not the hillock, and pass him by."
—A Civil War poem by S. A. Jones, "Only a Soldier's Grave"

CHAPTER 7

The field below Prospect Hill greened in the warming sun, the undisturbed grass masking thousands of shallow graves that had been hastily dug on a cold December morning in 1862. Harry stared at the wooded ridge, the line of trees wearing the most visible scars of the Battle of Fredericksburg. Charred trunks with skeletal limbs and sheared tops loomed dark and haunting against a bluing sky.

In the end, Harry was grateful that John Laird and Jamie had accompanied him and Elijah on the first leg of the trip South. Not one to leave his farm, John had recently heard the story of a family from Gray, Maine, who picked up their son's burial container at the Portland station. Before his interment, the grief-stricken parents had opened the casket to take a last look at their son, only to find the body of an unknown soldier in a Confederate gray uniform. Believing that the soldier's family would want a proper burial, and hoping someone would do the same for their son, they buried the soldier in the town's cemetery. Months later, when their son's body was at last identified, they brought him home and laid him at rest not far from the Confederate stranger. John knew that Leighton's parents, Leonard and Mabel, old and quite frail, lost without their only child, could not as easily handle receiving a mistaken casket. As their friend, he felt an obligation to go to Fredericksburg and to keep

Leighton's casket under his watchful eyes until it arrived in Berwick. In turn, the grateful pair had insisted on paying John's travel. Jamie's teacher Mary, believing Jamie would learn more on this single trip than in her schoolroom, urged John to let him go as well, and easily paid for his train fare.

"This where you fought, Harry?" asked Jamie as he ran to the edge of the battlefield, seeing only the tall grasses sprinkled with spring wildflowers, billowing blue in the breeze. Following his steps, Harry stared at the grassy field without seeing it, his mind invoking a different scene.

After hitching the horse and wagon to a tree, John and Elijah joined them at the road's edge.

"Tell me, Harry. Tell me what happened," Jamie urged.

Harry drew a long breath. "We crossed the Rappahannock River over yonder under a hailstorm of fire. Most of the 17th moved along there, the Richmond Stage Road," he said, turning and pointing his finger. "We were in front of another unit, Pennsylvanians, I think, who were plum worn out and had little ammunition left. Anyways, we drove the Georgia regiment back."

"So you won, you won!" Jamie's face widened with excitement.

Harry turned to all of them. "We fought well, scattered the enemy in the woods. Things was fairly quiet for a few hours, then by late afternoon, the Rebels charged again, and let loose their rifles on us. Came right out of that wooded ridge. We was dodging shells and artillery. Officers shouted for us to go prone. We were right out there," he said, his voice halting. "Leighton was always slow as molasses. Didn't drop to the ground fast enough. Took a bullet to his chest."

Harry walked over to the open trench where he had spent a bitter cold night lying across dried cornstalks and wheat rubble in the half-frozen mud, listening to the mournful cries of the wounded strewn across the bloodied field. In the early dawn, there had been a short truce to collect the wounded and bury the dead. Harry, Charlie, and Josh had rushed to bury Leighton.

Harry scanned the horizon, singling in on a massive oak tree across the field. Though half burned and missing most of its once-sprawling lower limbs, the majestic oak still stood, and using it as a vantage point, Harry told the others that Leighton's grave was about three hundred paces into the field. "The oak tree," he said as he pointed his finger, "will be our line of sight." He stepped off the road and moved into the field.

"I'll pace it out. Spread out on either side of me but don't stray too far from your side of the oak."

Harry took the lead. Across the field, emerging from the woods from where the Rebels had made their late afternoon advance, he spotted three men and wondered if they were also hoping to reclaim a friend's remains, tracking as he was, given their point of origin.

Harry shouted out each pace, and as soon as he reached two hundred, he urged his companions to move more slowly, allowing time to part the high grass and begin looking for a small cluster of stones. Beneath his feet, the uneven ground was his constant reminder that their footsteps tread on hallowed ground.

Throughout the search, Harry kept an occasional eye on the three strangers, and became increasingly concerned when it appeared they were making little effort to look for a grave. In fact, the men were now rapidly closing the distance between them. "Rebels," he muttered out loud, "coming right at me again."

"John, Elijah," he called, "might have some trouble afoot. Some fellas coming from the Confederate side of the field making a beeline for us."

John stopped, noticed the men for the first time, and turned to Jamie. "Son, I want you back on the wagon now!" There was no mistaking his pa's tone; Jamie turned and ran to the wagon.

"Morning, fellas," said Harry as the three approached. He guessed that two of the men were about his age, and the third perhaps a good ten years older or more.

"Looking to retrieve a body?" asked the older in a gruff tone.

"Yes, sir. A friend is buried out here."

One of the younger men took a step forward. "You 'all been looking where them Yanks fell. Reckon that makes you 'all Yanks, except for your slave."

"He ain't no slave. No cause to say that," Harry angrily replied. "The war's over."

"Not for us it ain't," said the older man, shaking his head. "Ain't that right, Clemons?"

"It's a long way from over," Clemons answered. He cast an angry face at Harry. "You Yanks did more'n enough damage down here. Going to take time to put things right, if we ever can."

"We'll find our friend and be gone."

"You was here—fighting—weren't you?" asked the older man, crinkling his brow.

Harry hesitated, nodded his head. "And you?"

"The three of us fought on this here field. Between us we got us a whole lot of friends buried out yonder, including my younger brother."

Harry raked his fingers through his dark hair. "I'm right sorry."

"Not enough time to mark the location of all of the bodies, so we struggle with just having to leave them be. Can't expect us to take kindly to you 'all tearing up this ground. This field's a graveyard now."

"Understand. But I know right where to look. If it's any comfort, you'll have one less Yank left on your soil." Harry placed his hands on his hips. "Now, please, and I don't mean to be rude, but if you'll excuse us, we've got our business to take care of."

The three men stood, unmoving.

The air grew heavy with silence. Seconds ticked away.

"Not a day goes by that I don't recall what happened here," Harry said at last. "Wakes me up at night. Then I see it all again, the fighting, like I was still here." He looked out across the battlefield. "Fredericksburg was my first engagement. Has a way of staying with you."

"Soldier's heart," said the older man. His dark eyes clouded, but his tone had softened. "Clemons here," he said, "he's haunted all the time."

"I guess we understand one another, then."

"Do at that."

The men retreated across the field, slowly fading from view as a bank of fast-moving clouds hovered like a slate blanket over the tall grasses.

"Let's get going," Harry said at last. Waving his arm toward the wagon, Harry beckoned Jamie back onto the field.

"What'd he mean, 'soldier's heart'?" asked John.

Harry took a long, deep breath. "Army docs near the end of the war give it the name. It's when you can't get the fighting out of your mind. Your head, your heart, feel like a whipped dog."

They paced, parted the grass, and studied the ground for an hour, yet none of the hidden earthen mounds claimed a pile of stones.

Suddenly, sweat dripping from his brow, John shouted, "I've found what appears to be a grave with stones fairly scattered around it."

Rushing over, Harry dropped down on his knees and examined each of the stones, rolling them over in his hands. "This one here's got a distinct line of quartz. I figured it would be easier to recognize." He glanced up at his landmark oak across the field. "Looks about right. This is the grave. Let's dig."

"Hand me the shovel," John said to Elijah. "I'll dig. Fetch the wagon, if you will." He turned to his son. "And you go with him. I want you to stay on the buckboard. I'm sorry, Jamie, but this ain't going to be a pretty sight."

Harry looked at John, nodded in approval. "This won't take long, Mr. Laird. No one had time to dig deep. Truce only lasted two hours."

"How can you be sure the body we find will be Leighton's?"

"Pinned his name to the inside of his coat pocket. Lots of us did that just before the battle, afraid no one would identify us."

John pushed the shovel into the earth. Harry was right. Skeletal remains were quickly found. With great tenderness they brushed the loosened soil from the decomposed corpse, careful to save the remnants of the soiled dark blue cloth that was his uniform. Harry searched for the coat pocket, pushed the dirt aside, and reached inside. He pulled out a limp scrap of yellowed paper. *Leighton Tasker, Berwick, Maine.* "It's him. We found you, Leighton." Gently touching the remains, Harry breathed deeply and said, "You're going home, my friend."

When the wagon arrived, Elijah jumped down and pulled the burial container out from the tailboard. He stood silently as John and Harry gently lifted the skeletal remains, pieces of uniform, and Leighton's cap into the box. Suddenly Harry leaned over, picked up the cap, brushed away the dirt, and stuffed it into his pocket. "Reckon Leighton's folks might want this."

They closed the lid and stepped back while Elijah began filling the emptied hole.

"Stop, Elijah!" Harry shouted, dropping down on his knees. "I thought I saw something." Sifting the dirt through his fingers, he held a spent bullet up for the others to see.

"This here's what brought him down. This is for me to keep." He hurriedly raked his fingers deeper into the loose soil, found nothing else. "I kept his haversack for a time. Lost it somewhere along the way. Still, it's good to check for something we might have missed when we buried him." At last Harry got back on his feet, shook the dirt from his trousers, and nodded to Elijah, who filled and packed the emptied grave.

*"Learning of Lee's surrender, he went the next day to
Richmond and there rejoiced with the victorious, but with
pity for the vanquished brave, he visited and talked hopefully
with the Confederate prisoners."*
—Emeline Cheney, *The Story of the Life and Work of Oren B. Cheney*

CHAPTER 8

Oren Cheney looked his pocket watch. It was time to head for Libby Prison if he was going to make the 3:10 Richmond, Fredericksburg & Potomac train to Washington for the long journey back to Maine. During the past two days, he had visited Richmond's thirteen hospitals, which mercifully had been left intact while most of the city burned. He found the hospitals remarkably clean and well staffed by surgeons and nurses who attended to the more than four thousand sick and wounded. As he hurried down the hospital corridor, he came to a sudden stop, startled at the sight of William Hurlin, a Freewill minister from Antrim, New Hampshire.

"William, my friend!" Oren clasped the reverend's hand and shook it warmly. "I heard you were somewhere in the South. What brings you to Richmond? "

"Why am I not surprised to find you here?" asked William, smiling. "My military service is over. I'm in Virginia as a volunteer delegate with the U.S. Christian Commission at Point of Rocks, not far from here. I had some free time and thought I would see firsthand the woeful destruction of this city."

"Come along with me, then. I'm on my way to Libby Prison."

Oren and William walked across the hospital grounds on Navy Hill and headed west to Water Street to the prison, where Union authorities still detained several hundred former Confederate officers.

Before entering the stark gray building, Oren pointed to the sign attached to the masonry wall: *L. Libby & Son, Ship Chandlers.* "Ironic," he said, "that one of the South's most infamous prisons is named after a Maine native, Luther Libby." Captain Libby had leased the building from the Enders family in 1854, and with the outbreak of the war, he had closed his business in Richmond but continued to maintain his lease. After the Battle of Bull Run, hundreds of prisoners were marched into Richmond. The Confederate Army commandeered Libby's building as well as many others for prisoner and hospital use. Events unfolded so quickly that no one had taken down the sign, and the former chandlery became known as Libby Prison. When Richmond fell, the Federals immediately used the vacated prison to hold Confederate officers slated to be tried for crimes of war.

Oren made known their intentions to the officer of the day, who gave them permission to see the prisoners, but admonished Oren to keep the visit brief. William, standing to the side, spotted a large, unopened packing crate stashed against the wall. The words sprawled across the top caught his immediate attention: *American Bible Society, New York.*

"Excuse me, officer, but may I inquire as to the contents of this crate? It's from the American Bible Society."

"Found it here when we took over the prison a few weeks ago. You both being preachers, and all, you may as well open it." The officer retrieved an iron bar from the cabinet and handed it to them.

Wedging the bar under the tight wooden slats, William raised a plank enough for Oren to peer into the crate. "It's filled with small Testaments!"

"Imagine they were intended to be distributed to the Northern prisoners," said William.

"There's a pity," replied Oren. "But perhaps we can put them to good use now." Oren asked the officer if he could speak to the prison commandant. Minutes later, with the commandant's approval, Oren and William, their arms filled with the Testaments, headed for the stairwell.

As they ascended the dark, narrow stairway, the air became heavy with the stench of sweat and unwashed bodies. William turned quickly to Oren. "Whatever your intentions were here today with the prisoners, please know that I am just a passenger." Oren nodded. With each measured step, he felt his need had never been greater.

When the ministers reached the second floor landing, a guard greeted them and let them pass. The long room was overcrowded with men standing and sitting about on the floor; the air was fetid. Many flattened their faces against the barred windows, filling their lungs with fresh air all the while hoping to chance a glimpse of sunlight. As the two ministers moved purposefully into the hallway, the prisoners stared in curiosity yet eagerly accepted the Testaments. William made several trips up and down the stairs to gather more of the little books; Oren guessed they had distributed at least three hundred. As Oren offered greetings, faces scowled upon hearing his clipped northern accent.

"What business you Yankee preachers have here?" asked a senior officer, his beard streaked with lines of gray.

"We came to listen," Oren responded. And listen they did as they walked among the prisoners, hearing their collective outrage at the Federals' barbarous destruction of Richmond and their own anxieties about an uncertain future. Expecting to be tried for war crimes, the Confederate officers feared they would remain held in the foul, darkened rooms of Libby Prison for a very long time. What would become of their families? A sense of hopelessness pervaded the jail's rooms like a suffocating fog.

Finally, Oren stopped and positioned himself near the stairwell, where he reasoned he could be heard by most of the men. William stood close by, leaned his back against the wall. Oren called out to the prisoners, asking if he might speak to them. The men shuffled and squeezed together, curious to hear what a Yankee preacher could possibly offer them when all was lost, dreams shattered forever.

"I proposed to come to you that we might find spiritual comfort together—that I might impart some spiritual gift in this great time of need. I have listened with my heart to your sorrows and your sufferings, and I say to you in the words of Paul the Apostle, 'I consider that the sufferings of this present time are not worthy to be compared with the glory which shall be revealed in us.'" Oren took a fleeting glance around the room. "Do not lose hope, however far away and unobtainable it may seem. Lay open your hearts to God—"

"God abandoned us," cried a young man who leaned heavily on a crude wooden crutch, his left leg amputated below the knee. "Where is the hope?"

"Hope is lost!" another shouted from the back of the hallway, only to be echoed by a raucous chorus.

Oren studied the hardened faces. He spoke more slowly. "Do not walk away from so great a salvation, my friends. As you experience this time of trial and suffering, however heavy, however lost you may feel, you are never separated from God's love. You are masked in pain, and you do not see or feel God's love, but it dwells within you, and with patience you will find him again." Oren paused, as if waiting for another outcry, but the room was silent.

Then a voice called out, a smooth and refined voice befitting a southern gentleman of privilege. "Many of us will rot here while we wait to be tried. You speak of salvation. Salvation is for those who have not sinned against God; in his eyes are we not condemned?" Faces turned anxiously back to the northern minister.

Oren took a deep breath and with great tenderness said, "We are all sinners before God, but faith in Jesus Christ brings us forgiveness and he clothes us in a robe of righteousness. If you walk with the spirit of God, even with your enemies, then you will be saved. God will not abandon you."

Oren paused and, seeing a soldier wipe his eyes with the sleeve of his soiled and ragged coat, he walked over and stood before the man.

The soldier hung his head. "Pastor, I fear I've lost my way, my faith in God."

"We all lack faith sometimes. I know you have suffered many difficult and dark days, my son. May I ask your name?"

"Lieutenant Austin Shelby, sir."

"Take whatever faith remains within you, Lieutenant Shelby, and open your heart to God, for faith flows from our inmost being. Faith will show you the way back."

Oren raised his face to the crowd. "And to all who are imprisoned here, do not lose your faith, however thin and ragged it may be. Do not let it go. I declare unto you that faith and hope will remove the mountains before you. Paul said, 'there is no height, nor depth, nor any other creature, shall be able to separate us from the love of God.' If among us there are those who do not hold this faith, begin your journey now. Whatever the circumstance you are facing, God is willing to walk through it with you."

Lieutenant Shelby dropped down on bended knee. Oren rested his hand on the young officer's shoulder.

"Hear the word of God, and believe in him. Accept the salvation available in Jesus Christ, his most precious gift to us. Though you may see through a glass darkly now, there are three things that are never moved: faith, hope, and love. The greatest of these is God's love. It 'Beareth all things, believeth all things, hopeth all things, endureth all things.' God's love never fails."

A prison guard rushed up the stairs and admonished Oren, saying it was time for them to go.

Acknowledging his words, Oren looked at the guard and asked, "It saddens me that we must take our leave, but I ask if first I might pray together with these men?" The guard begrudgingly nodded approval and hurried back down the stairs.

Oren stood silently. In the immediate hush, two senior officers went down on their knees beside Lieutenant Shelby and bowed their heads. Suddenly there was a scurry of men trying to share the crowded space on bended knees, but a few stood tall, their arms crossed over their chests. Perhaps I've succeeded in reaching a few, Oren thought, as was my purpose. Bowing his head, he offered a final prayer.

As Oren and William exited Libby Prison, appreciative of the sun streaming on their faces, they heard voices calling to them. Looking up, they saw a number of small bags being lowered by strings from the upper floor windows. A few voices called out to them. "Testaments, please!"

"Oren, did we not reach all the prisoners?"

"Rather ingenious of them," said Oren as the bags landed near his feet. "Apparently there are more men on the third floor we were not made aware of. So great a need."

The ministers turned back and entered the prison. Within minutes, the guards gathered handfuls of Testaments still left in the crate and disappeared up the stairs.

"Expect I'll see you at the Yearly Meeting," said William as the two men parted.

"I'll see you in Northwood, my friend."

"We didn't know where to go or what to do."
—Daniel Waring, 88, emancipated slave, Federal Writers' Project,
National Humanities Center

CHAPTER 9

Taking leave from his friend, Oren walked the city streets, making his way to the depot. He shook his head at the wanton destruction of the massive flour mills along the banks of the James River. With the occupation of the federal forces, there was at last a sense of order in the war's aftermath, but his heart was heavy with the sights of Richmond's smoking ruins.

His spirits lifted when he rounded a corner and saw a cluster of emancipated slaves a short distance away walking freely about, jubilation still written across their faces. Eager to rejoice with them, and without hesitation, Oren called out, "Gentlemen, if I may?"

The men turned, stared warily as the refined-looking white man walked unabashedly toward them, a wide smile across his face. One of the men became visibly hostile, moved cautiously toward Oren, stopping a few feet in front of him. One hurriedly walked away, while another shook his head, shifted anxiously on his feet.

No one spoke.

Oren looked at their questioning faces, their hesitation. "Please, you have nothing to fear from me." He kept his voice low, his tone nonthreatening.

The hostile one spat onto the street, wiped his mouth with the back of his hand. "What you want, mistah? Ain't nuthin' here for you."

"I want only to share with you in your joy that you are free. I have always believed that slavery was a sin against God. And now he has delivered you from those who chose to enslave you."

"Lord, he do right," a new voice shouted from behind the others.

"You some kind of preacher man?" asked the hostile one.

"I'm a minister, from the North."

"Then why you here?"

"I was only passing through, and when I came around the corner and saw you all, I wanted to rejoice with you." Oren scanned their faces, and seeing their blank expressions, said, "Forgive me for disturbing your peace."

"You keep yourself moving on."

"Jules, he not so bad. Leave him be." A tall, slender man stepped out of the crowd and came to stand in front of Oren.

"Maybe this preacher got something to say."

"No white folk got nuthin' I want."

A bugle called in the distance. The hostile one stopped and, like the others, turned his face to its signaling sound.

"Still the bugle calls, but no longer a call to arms," said Oren with great emotion in his voice.

When the bugle ceased, Oren said quietly, "I'll move on."

"Preacher man, what we go and do now we all free?" asked the slender one.

"Is there no work in front of you?"

Their collective faces fell sharply, like shattered glass. Oren glanced at the hostile one, who stood unmoving, his arms crossed against his chest, but he remained silent.

"Don't know," said a new voice. He was a strapping man, and unlike the others, he was dressed in a dark suit and white shirt. Although his clothes looked worn and badly wrinkled, Oren guessed the man had at one time been a household servant in one of Richmond's finer neighborhoods. As if reading Oren's mind, the man said, "Used to work in the home of one of them bankers, but he done took off when the Yanks got near Richmond— sent me to one of them mill owners. Mills is burning to the ground, but the owner he tell me I can work, clearing the debris, but he ain't got no money to pay me right now, and don't knows when he can. So I just walking around with nowhere to go." He shook his head.

"We gots families to feed," pleaded another. "I go back to the mastuh and he tell me to git myself gone now I free. I was wanting to stay and work. At least I knows him. Hard to trust a white folk who a stranger."

"Even if he a preacher," added the hostile one, his tone still guarded. "We only ever work in the city. Never picked no cotton, no tobacco."

"Don't know, just don't know."

"We free, but we ain't got nowheres to go."

"Go but to God," Oren said softly.

"What you say, preacher man? Ain't you got nuthin' to give us?"

Oren heard the anguish in their voices. "I'm reminded of what the apostle Peter said, 'As a man of the cloth, silver and gold have I none, but such as I have to give, I give you God's word.'"

"What word be that?" The men gathered around him, their faces searching for more.

"That you are not lost from God. He has not forgotten you. When the day comes, tomorrow or the next, God will take you by the hand and lift you up."

"How that be?"

"He hears us through prayer and then speaks to us through His word, which will be a light unto His path. I will gladly lead you in prayer if you'd like."

The men glanced in silence at each other until the hostile one grudgingly nodded his assent.

Oren reached in his pocket, opened a small Testament he had kept for himself, and leafing through the pages stopped and read from the book of Philippians. After he finished, he prayed with them.

"I must be going," he said at last. "Know that God is with you."

"He hear us now?"

"He will speak to you."

The train depot bustled with activity. Federals scurried to unload hundreds of crates from the overburdened cars and onto waiting supply wagons. The conductor, at last calling for boarding, announced the train would be late in arriving at Fredericksburg, and as a result, passengers changing rail lines would experience an additional delay. It would be a long journey home. Oren sighed as he settled into his seat and closed his eyes.

He thought for a moment about Luther. Was I prosperous these past two days? he asked himself.

A few hours later the train whistled its approach to the Fredericksburg station. Restless, with time on his hands, Oren strolled along the platform.

Nearing the end of the line, he was about to turn and head back to his car when he came upon two men, a boy, and a colored man standing beside a casket. He caught his breath. In large letters, the burial container was marked "Berwick, Maine."

"Excuse me gentlemen," Oren asked. "I see this casket is going to Maine?"

John Laird glanced at the dignified looking man and nodded. "One of our boys, a friend. Killed here, at Fredericksburg."

Offering his condolences, Oren bowed his head momentarily, and then turning to them, made his introduction. "I ministered not far from you, at the Freewill Baptist Church in Lebanon, for several years."

"Guess that makes you our neighbor. I'm John Laird and this is Harry, my son Jamie, and our friend, Elijah. Pleased to meet you Reverend—"

"Cheney, Oren Cheney."

Harry's eyes brightened. "I've heard your name. If I remember, you raised the money to build Lebanon Academy. My betrothed taught there for a few months 'til the teaching job opened up in Berwick. You still there?"

Oren shook his head. "My home is in Lewiston now." Glancing at the four of them, he said, "I'm pleased to make this unexpected acquaintance. Are you all taking the train back?"

"Only Mr. Laird and Jamie," answered Harry. "Elijah and I have other business down here."

"Elijah lives with us, and he's coming back home, but first he's going to look for his pa somewheres," Jamie added. "And Harry's going to look for Josh."

"Another casualty of war?"

Harry shook his head. "I'm hoping not. He was taken prisoner. I'm going to Salisbury to look for him."

"And your father, Elijah?"

"He not far from Salisbury. Elijah—"

Suddenly the conductor's voice boomed. "Load that casket into the car," he shouted testily, "and get on board. Train's ready to pull out."

"Forgive me for holding you up," Oren said.

"Excuse me, Reverend," said John, grabbing one end of the burial container as Harry reached for the other. "Perhaps my son and I will see you on the train."

"Delighted. I'm in the third car."

Oren watched somberly as the two men carefully lifted and slid the casket onto the emptied car, pushing it into the corner. Turning first to Harry, he said, "I sincerely hope you find your friend. And you, your father, Elijah."

"Thanks, Reverend," said Harry. "I can't wait to tell Mary I met you. And here of all places."

"Mr. Cheney, suh?" Elijah turned a shy face to him.

"Yes, my son?"

"Maybe you say a prayer for Elijah? Help Elijah find Pappy."

"It would be my privilege, Elijah. God hears and answers prayer."

*"There are stars whose light only reaches the earth long after
they have fallen apart. There are people whose remembrance
gives light in this world long after they have passed away. This
light shines in our darkest nights on the road we must follow."*
—The Talmud

CHAPTER 10

After parting with Oren Cheney and the Lairds, Harry and Elijah
took the next train to Richmond, and when inquiring about
their connections, learned they would be taking the Richmond
& Danville line into Danville, Virginia. From there, however, with the
Piedmont line to North Carolina not yet finished, they were distressed to
learn, they would need to walk nearly ninety miles to Salisbury. In spite
of the cold stares and occasional harsh murmurings of a few passengers
directed at Elijah, the trip was mercifully uneventful.

It was mid-afternoon when the train pulled into the Danville
station. Aware that only a few miles separated him from Master Fowler's
plantation, Elijah kept a watchful eye when he stepped onto the station
platform. Images of Buckra, the brutal overseer, raced through his mind,
and he flinched when he felt a strong tug on his arm.

"Elijah," Harry said. "Did you hear me?"

"No, suh. Elijah thinking about Buckra. Maybe slave catchers here.
We gots to move on."

"Leastways you're not alone now. We've food enough for a couple of
days. Ain't no need to buy provisions here. Conductor says the road we're
looking for is right off the station—over there."

As they approached the road leading out of town, Elijah grew
anxious; his skin pricked with fear. He turned to Harry. "Bad feeling,
suh. They eyes on me."

Harry scanned the landscape, trying to separate the flurry of activity in the busy railroad town from folks going about their business to anything that seemed strange, out of place. Were there men watching or following them? Although he saw nothing to unsettle him, he understood Elijah's fear. He would have to remember to be more cautious.

"Most likely your mind's scaring up demons, us being so close and all, Elijah. But I'm thinking we ought to head into the woods. We'll follow the road just the same; at least we'll be out of sight."

Shortly after ducking into the line of trees that edged the road, they spotted what looked to be a deer path that meandered through thick stands of alder, cedar, ash, and oak. They came upon a creek bed, cupped their hands in the cool water, drank thirstily, and refilled their flasks. Moving on, and staying under the cover of trees, they listened to the raucous chattering of the crows softened only occasionally by the sweet warbling of songbirds in the thrushes.

Even as the sun dipped behind the western hills the air remained mild, and they found the trek almost agreeable in spite of the long miles ahead. Still wary of his surroundings, Elijah embraced each measured step that distanced him farther and farther from Fowler's long reach. They walked most of the time in silence, speaking only when necessary, using hand signals when their path brought them too close to the road. Elijah took comfort in Harry's unruffled confidence as he led them through the woods and fields, his skill no doubt learned during his years in the army. His initial impression of Harry had not disappointed him, and during the long train ride from Maine Harry had used the time to ask about Billy. It surprised Elijah how easy it was to talk to Harry. "He bring you along," mused Elijah. "He bring you along."

The forest gradually opened onto an endless rolling pasture lush with spring grasses. In the dimming light Harry spotted the main road, the thick stand of woods on the other side. In spite of the absence of travelers, he signaled Elijah with his hand to head across the road.

"Going to be dark soon," Harry said, relieved to be back under the cover of trees. "We'll get ourselves a little deeper in these woods, and then make camp for the night. Figured there may be cows moving out to that pasture we were in come morning."

Harry paced his steps as a way to judge their distance from the road. When they happened upon a small but fast-moving stream, a mossy clearing near its banks, Harry said they would settle for the night. He decided against a fire. "We'll dry camp. Once we're out of this farmland, I'll feel better about a fire." They ate a meal of dried beef and biscuits, refilled their flasks, spread their wool blankets, and slept soundly on the cool, soft moss.

For the next two days they kept to the woods and the occasional cow paths through overgrown pasturelands. They traveled more slowly when the underbrush became so thick, and they occasionally had to stop and untangle themselves from the brambles.

On their third day out, just before dark, they came upon a stream and a grassy clearing wide enough to offer an unobstructed view of the sky.

"Let's make camp early and enjoy the night," said Harry, pleased with the site. "Didn't see farms all day, so I reckon it's safe enough to build us a fire."

Elijah scraped out a small pit and gathered stones to make a fire ring; Harry retreated into the woods, returning with his arms filled with dried pine limbs and bits of kindling. It felt good to sit by a fire and enjoy its warmth, and, after a light meal, they sat in lingering, comfortable silence.

"What'll you do if you find your father?" Harry asked later as he tossed a handful of broken limbs into the fire pit. "You plannin' on bringing him back to Maine?"

Elijah shrugged his shoulders. "Mostly Elijah need to see him, know he all right. Pappy may think Elijah even dead."

"If you stay on here, I'm thinking Jamie will be moving on down." Harry chuckled. "That boy's mighty fond of you. Plain as day."

Elijah only shook his head and smiled.

Darkness walked through the forest and a chilling breeze wormed its way around the trees.

Shaking their blankets, they settled down on the grass on opposite sides of the fire.

"Billy and me was always looking at them stars," Elijah said as he cradled his head in his hands.

"Yeah, lot like I done. All those nights during the war, sleeping on the ground. Most times without a tent. Used to say them stars was my only cover." Harry scanned the sky. "Hey, look straight up! A shooting star!"

"Yes, suh, sure enough. Billy, suh, he say when them stars fall out of the sky they make a big ol' hole in the ground."

"Aw, Billy," Harry reflected. "Don't surprise me none he would say something like that."

"He say them stars just plum wore out."

"Maybe so, Elijah, maybe so. Did you know that when you see a shooting star you make a wish on it?"

"Then Elijah make one. Elijah wish Pappy be fine."

"And I'll wish for my friend Josh," Harry added as he rolled over onto his side, wrapping himself in his blanket. "Let's get some rest now."

"The spirit which made him a pioneer among our people in getting an education for himself made him a pioneer in securing the opportunities for an education for others. It meant faith in the night, patience under criticism, persistency when hope has fled, and all the energies of his remaining public life, but to this he was consecrated..."
—Reverend Thomas Hobbs Stacy on Oren Cheney,
The Morning Star, July 14, 1898

CHAPTER 11

"An unspeakable tragedy, John," said Oren Cheney. "I remember reading in the paper that a private from the 17th Maine had been executed at Fort Preble. I thought that was in itself unusual, to face a firing squad here, but I had no idea of the circumstances surrounding your son's death. I'm so very sorry."

"He's with God. He's at peace."

"He is that." For a long moment Oren stared out the window, a sense of renewal filling his soul as the meadows rolling past him bloomed in splashes of spring colors. When he turned back, he saw Jamie reading *Walden.*

Aware of Oren's eyes upon him, Jamie looked up and said, "Elijah and me was reading this before we come South."

"So Elijah reads?"

"Only some. I've been learning him. I read the first two chapters to him 'cause Miss Rogers, that's my teacher, said we need to tell her why Thoreau went and lived in the woods. Elijah understood why Thoreau went better'n me."

"Perhaps because he has had to live without the pleasures we all enjoy."

"Yeah. He told me if you got freedom, you don't need much more."

"So Elijah has been with you all since—"

"Since my brother died," Jamie said, finishing the sentence. "Him and Billy was on the Underground Railroad together. Then Elijah went to Canada. But he come back to see Billy that next summer. He said Billy wanted him to be my big brother." Jamie let out a long sigh. "But Elijah and me, it's like he was always my brother."

Placing an arm on Jamie's shoulder, John gave his son an easy hug.

"You remind me a little of myself, Jamie, when I was your age," Oren said.

"How you figure?"

"Well, for most of my childhood I lived in New Hampshire. My parents used our home to shelter runaway slaves on the way to Canada."

"Just like the Underground Railroad?" Jamie's eyes widened with excitement.

"Yes, our home was one of the stations."

"So you had lots of slaves stay with you?"

Oren nodded. "By the time I was your age my father would let me lead them part of the way to the next station."

Jamie looked up and stared at Oren. "Thunder! Slaves been escaping that long?"

Oren laughed. "Yes, it's been over thirty years since I lived in Peterborough. But slaves were escaping even long before that. And over the years, when circumstances allowed, I continued to harbor runaway slaves."

John leaned into the conversation. "In Maine as well?"

Oren nodded. "I was principal and preacher of Parsonsfield Seminary in 1843 for a few years. While I was there, I used my home as a station. Most of the runaways that arrived in Parsonsfield came from Portland, and then went on to their next shelter in Effingham Hill."

"Didn't Parsonsfield Seminary burn to the ground?" asked John.

"Indeed, in 1854. Its burning disturbed me greatly. When I heard the news one evening, I became deeply concerned about the numbers of young people scattered throughout Maine's villages and farms without the means of obtaining a good education. I paced well into the night, and just before dawn I envisioned founding a new school. It was as if God said, *Do this work for me.* It was to be my life's calling, the founding of an educational institution that would serve Maine and beyond. I held a pastorate in Augusta at the time, and the next day I resigned, believing God had entrusted me with the education of young people."

"But I thought there was no new school built to replace the one in Parsonsfield?"

"You are correct about that, John. I felt strongly that the school I envisioned should be more centrally located in the state. Three years after what I refer to as my divine call, in 1857, the Maine State Seminary in Lewiston enrolled its first students."

"And you are its leader?" asked John.

Oren nodded. "Yes, I am the president."

Jamie flung down his book. "Pa, I want to go the seminary!"

"And I should love to have you as a student someday," said Oren smiling. "But it's no longer called the Maine State Seminary. We have a collegiate department now, and have changed our name to honor our major benefactor, Benjamin Bates."

Jamie shrugged his shoulders. "Then what's it called?"

"Bates College."

*"I am the LORD your God, who brought you out of the land
of Egypt, that you should not be their slaves; I have broken
the bands of your yoke and made you walk upright."*
—Leviticus 26:13

CHAPTER 12

Harry startled awake when he heard Elijah shout. A shadowy-looking figure hovered over him, and then pushed the muzzle of his rifle into his chest.

"Don't you move none." In the gray dawn light, Harry blinked hard at the loathsome-looking stranger. An oily beard speckled with crusted dirt and bits of dried food framed the man's hollowed face. Harry's first thought was of Elijah; he snapped his head to his left, only to see Elijah face down in the dirt and another man, younger and plumper than the first, tying Elijah's hands behind him. Then he braced his foot heavily on Elijah's back. Elijah raised his head; his eyes, dark with fear, met Harry's. Harry sucked in his breath; three long years of fighting had taught him to work through his fear, to train his mind to think and act clearly. "We'll be okay, Elijah," he stammered.

"See you ain't no slave catcher," the man said, "or this here darkie would've been bound up. What're you doing with him no how?"

"Ain't no business of yours. He's a free man now."

"Well, some of us still on slave patrol. Catching old runaways. He got a pass from his employer say he freed?" Scowling, the man pressed the muzzle hard on Harry's ribs.

Harry winced at the pressure bearing down on him, but shook it off. "He doesn't need a pass. I said the man was free."

"Don't you go and git all high and mighty, boy. This here runaway's going with me."

Harry stared fiercely at him. "If it's money you want for him then take what I got. Just let us go."

"I think you're talking too much, boy."

"What will we do with him?" asked the man's partner, brushing sweat from his brow, leaving streaks of dirt across his wide forehead. Harry thought he seemed almost frightened, unsure of himself.

"We don't mean you no trouble. Like I said, take my money and let us go," Harry offered again.

"I'll take your money all right, but I reckon you won't be going anywhere. Except this darkie, he's coming with us. Caleb, go on and git the horses."

Harry watched Caleb disappear into the woods. Only one of them to deal with now, he thought, but he knew he couldn't do it alone, not with a rifle bearing down on him. He stole a glance at Elijah, who stared back with fierce resolve. Ever so slightly, Harry nodded his head, rolled his eyes in the stranger's direction, and nudged his shoulder forward. Understanding registered on Elijah's face.

Elijah did not hesitate. Pushing his knees under him, he thrust his muscled shoulders at the man, the unexpected force sending the musket flying out of his hands. Harry dove for the rifle. But the man quickly regained his balance and lunged at Harry. Their bodies collided, rolling and tumbling over the ground.

Pummeling Harry, the man struck him repeatedly in the gut with wrenching force. Bile rose in Harry's throat; he doubled over his stomach. Ignoring the pain, he used the position to garner the force of an upward thrust, and in an instant, he rammed a fisted hand into the man's jaw. *Crack!* The man fell, his limp body knocked unconscious. Harry exhaled, unaware he had been holding his breath. Racing to Elijah, he untied the rope that bound his hands, turned, and grabbed the musket.

A horse whinnied.

Caleb stood in the clearing, his rifle leveled at Elijah's head. "Put the musket down or I'm gonna shoot him."

"You don't want to do that, Caleb," said Harry, wiping his lips with the back of his hand. "Just let us go. Your friend's going to be all right."

He saw Caleb tremble, his finger loosen slightly on the trigger. Doubting Caleb had ever killed a man, Harry hoped he could talk him into letting them go. He remembered his own hesitation, early on in the war, when he was forced to fire his weapon at an advancing Confederate just yards away. That enemy soldier was young, like him, and his eyes were as blue as the sky above the battlefield. After that, Harry always found it easier to fire when he didn't see their faces.

Harry blew out a breath. "You work for him?"

"Digger's a partner, is all. Mr. Fowler's overseer hired us. Fowler's got a big tobacco farm around these parts. Some of his slaves took off afore they was freed, and now there ain't enough help to work the fields. His overseer, Buckra, told us to find some runaways before the law catches up with what he's doing. Now you put that rifle down."

Elijah shivered. Buckra, the devil himself. He knew Buckra would sooner kill him than put him to work again for Fowler. Adrenaline pulsed through him; he was ready to make his move.

Digger stirred, and touching his broken jaw, warped with pain, he let out a low moan.

Caleb shot a glance at Digger and in that fleeting second, Elijah thrust his body at him, pinning him face-down onto the ground.

Digger plunged into action, and rolling over onto his side, he reached for Caleb's loose rifle, leveled it point blank at Harry, and fired.

Like a seasoned soldier, Harry reacted quickly and dove to his left, the bullet exploding into the yellow pine behind him. He returned the fire, striking Digger in the chest. Digger dropped to the ground, his blood mingling with the earth beneath him.

"You killed him!" Caleb screamed, spitting dirt and dust from his mouth. "Don't shoot me. Please don't shoot me."

"You try and follow us, or come hunting us down with your boss, then I'll do what I have to do. Call it unfinished business, you and me." Harry stood over Digger's body and then turned his face to the morning sun, thirstily taking in large gulps of cool, crisp air.

His breathing slowed, he turned to Caleb. "You tell your boss that thieves killed Digger when he was sleeping. Didn't see you 'cause you were down by the creek. You got that?"

Caleb nodded. "I didn't want no part of this. Needing money, is all. Didn't figure on folks being harmed."

Elijah spewed rage at Caleb's words. "You go and take us coloreds back to Fowler and you thinking there be no harm? Buckra, he evil!"

"I wasn't meaning—you know him? Digger thought he'd seen you afore."

"Say no more." Harry kicked the musket aside. "Elijah, you take this one; I'll keep Digger's."

Trembling still, Elijah picked up the musket.

"Tell your boss the thieves took both the rifles. Tracks out of camp was heading west," Harry said as he picked the blankets up from the ground and kicked loose dirt into the fire pit.

"What'll I do with Digger?"

"Bury him. Bury him unless you want to carry him all the way back."

"I got his horse."

"Not any more. Thieves took it."

Letter from William Still to B. McKiernon. *"...he regained the God-given blessings of liberty. He eagerly sought his parents and home with all possible speed and pains, when to his heart's joy, he found his relatives."*
—William Still, African American abolitionist,
The Underground Railroad

CHAPTER 13

Harry and Elijah rode in uninterrupted silence for several miles. Anxious to shake the early morning's violence from his thoughts, Harry tried to focus on the rest of the day. "Don't worry none if we see some riders," he said. "We're sitting on these horses like we belong on them. Folks ain't going to be wondering what we're up to. Horses give us that."

Elijah only nodded, no longer sure he had the emotional strength to get through another encounter with vengeful white folk. While he had been both victim and witness to inhuman acts in his past, he'd never seen a man shot before, and in spite of the sun's warmth bearing down on his back, he could not shake the chill that penetrated his soul.

Sensing Elijah's distress, Harry said, "I didn't like killing that man. But it was him or me. Seen enough of war to know a man can't hesitate."

"Yes, suh."

"You ain't never seen a man shot before?"

Elijah shook his head no.

"When I mustered, I tried to prepare myself for what was to come. Never got the chance. Just four months down South and we was fighting in Fredericksburg. First battle, I saw my good friend shot. After that, I kept telling myself it was the enemy or me. Those fellas this morning, Elijah, they was the enemy this time. We had no choice."

"Yes, suh."

"By the way, thanks for not hesitating. Things might have turned out different otherwise. If you was a soldier, I'd be right proud to have you by my side." Harry turned in his saddle, and seeing the pain still etched on Elijah's face, said, "I'll leave you alone with your thoughts. Just think on what I said."

They rode again in silence, each lost in his own meditations, the only sound the clopping hooves on the hard-packed road. A pair of riders were at last spotted in the distance, heading toward them. The two slowed their horses as they approached, but did not stop. The older man, whose tufts of graying hair curled below his hat, offered a pleasantry and then urged his horse to move along. With barely a second glance, they were soon lost behind the curve in the road.

Harry glanced at Elijah. "Figure we have near sixty miles ahead of us. Mighty glad we have us these horses now. Reckon we'll be at your pa's in two days' time."

They rode the next day without incident, and on the morning of the second day, Elijah became visibly anxious; he was at once excited, at once fearful of what he might find.

"I'm riding to the farm with you, Elijah, and if your pa's there, I'll move on. It's a right warm night, so I'll sleep under the stars. I'll need to take your horse with me, for Josh. Should be back in a couple of days."

The hours crawled, the day sliding slowly into sundown. When Elijah saw the distant western hills, his senses heightened. He smelled the farmlands, the ripe overturned earth, before he saw the fields of his boyhood. He felt immediately a connection with the land, an attachment that even its harsh history could not purge.

"Harry, suh," he said breathlessly, pointing to the road as it curved sharply to the left, "Mastuh Ramsey's farm around this bend."

"Well, I'll be danged; we made it. By the way, Elijah, don't you call him master no more. You're as free as Ramsey now, and no man owns you."

"What I call him then?"

"Got me lots of names I'm wanting to call him," he said. "But you say mister, or sir. Just don't be saying master."

As they rounded the bend, the dense undergrowth of woody vines and patchwork of hickory, maple, and oak opened to a wide expanse of working fields. On either side, laborers, both white and colored, many of them children, empty seed bags hanging off their shoulders, appeared to be gathering their farm tools and heading for the distant barn, a long row of cabins edging its yard.

Leaning over the saddle horn, his heartbeat quickening, Elijah scanned the vast landscape as the horses plodded along the road. By the time they were more than halfway there, the fields had nearly emptied of workers and Elijah had still had not spotted his father. He tried to ignore the panic welling within him.

"Maybe he's in his cabin," offered Harry.

Elijah halted the reins, eased the horse around, and stopped. Shadows deepened over the fields as the lowering sun disappeared behind a tumble of clouds.

"You see him?"

Elijah shook his head. "Pappy always the last one on the fields, tending to them like they was his alone."

Trying to still his growing anxiety, Harry studied the farmlands and wondered how many slaves it had taken to farm the seemingly endless stretch of working fields.

Several agonizing minutes passed.

Elijah stirred nervously, turning his head in either direction, beads of sweat trickling down his back. He saw only a flock of crows scouring the vacated farmlands, their incessant cackling breaking the unsettling silence.

"We go to the cabin now, Harry, suh," he finally said, his voice choked with dread. Swiveling in his saddle, he took a last, lingering gaze.

And then he was off his horse, running, half-stumbling across the fields.

A lone figure, his hair snowy-white, clutched his hoe as he stepped cautiously across the rows. His gaze clearly fixed on the ground, he stopped abruptly as if considering one of the newly seeded rows, bent over, and with the back side of his hoe, tenderly patted the earth and moved on.

"Pappy! Pappy!"

Elijah's father raised his head and stared at the once familiar figure running toward him. Even in the fading sunlight, Harry saw the look of shock and disbelief flash across the older man's face.

The hoe slipped from his hands as if it were a weighted sack he could no longer hold on to. And then he dropped down to his knees, his arms hugging his chest.

Grabbing the reins of Elijah's horse, Harry let loose a sigh of relief, turned the horses around and headed down the road, disappearing behind its bend. "Let them be," he said to himself. "The war did some things right after all."

"I sought my soul
But my soul I could not see
I sought my God
But my God eluded me
I sought my brother
And I found all three"
—William Blake, *I Sought My Soul*

CHAPTER 14

Harry picked up the rail line and followed it south to Salisbury, judging it to be not more than ten miles away. Weary from the long day, he rode until he spotted a stone bridge over a creek, and veering away from the tracks, he made his bed beside the water's edge.

He woke early, watered the horses in the creek, and made his way again along the rails. Two hours had passed when his nostrils filled with the smell of smoke. As the sweet, sickly odor grew stronger, his horse slowed and whinnied. Harry urged the reluctant horse forward. His instincts told him something was wrong, but he refused to let his mind conjure dangerous, foreboding thoughts. As he rounded the track's last curve, he stared at piles of scorched ruins, the long stretch of blackened meadows. It was the prison compound; he could feel it.

Nothing remained except a small cottage on the edge of the field, remarkably untouched by the fires. The wooden stockade that once surrounded the prison was nothing more than a line of charred timbers, the last vestiges of its embers curling tufts of acrid smoke into the air. Dismounting, Harry tied the nervous horses near the small farmhouse and walked the perimeter until he found an opening he could safely walk through. The large oak trees in the center of the deserted compound, although blackened from the fires, survived. Beneath them stood a scorched brick building, its hollowed windows casting a haunting feel to the already forbidding landscape. What happened here? he pondered. What happened to Josh, the other prisoners?

Walking through the rubble, Harry searched for clues, anything that could shed light on the mysterious fire, but he found only ash and ruins. He had a sinking feeling in his gut, and for the first time he allowed himself to believe that he would not be taking Josh home. Josh. The little fellow with a big heart. Josh had been inconsolable after Leighton's death. Harry took him under his wing, but the inner light in Josh had dimmed, the horrors of war killing his soul. Early one morning near Petersburg, orders came to advance through a cornfield, leaving the soldiers no protection except the stalks. He remembered the bullets whistling through the air, cutting the cornstalks like a scythe. Josh was lost in the hail of smoke and fire, and when the fighting had ended, he was nowhere to be found. Harry later learned that the Rebels had taken a few prisoners not far from the area where he believed Josh to be. Weeks passed before Harry learned Josh was a prisoner of war in Salisbury.

Harry walked dejectedly from the compound. Perhaps in Salisbury he would learn the fate of the Union prisoners. Standing by the horses was a pleasant looking woman, her auburn hair coiled and netted. Smiling shyly at him, she offered a greeting and said she lived in the house near what was once the prison's main gates.

Harry tipped his cap and said, "Ma'am. Harry Warren. I'm looking for a friend who was held here. Came looking for him, but I see it's all burned down. Sure would like to know what happened, and what became of the prisoners."

"Hello, Mr. Warren. I'm Sarah Johnson. The prisoners have been gone since February last. The prison was built to hold twenty-five hundred men, but by early last fall, it was forced to house nearly ten thousand. Conditions became deplorable." When Harry did not respond, she continued. "The Union Naval blockade caused a shortage of medicine and medical supplies. You can imagine the terrible suffering that went on, and all the needless deaths. Eventually all the buildings that housed the men were taken over for hospital use, and for the rest of the winter, the prisoners had no real shelter. Some even dug burrows in the ground to try and escape the cold."

Sarah took a few steps forward and stared out across the ruins. "Folks in town did what they could to help feed and clothe them."

Harry nodded. "I'm mighty glad to hear that."

"We weren't insensitive to their plight. And we did what we could. But conditions continued to worsen. I asked the prison commandant if I could help in any way that I could. Soldiers on both sides were sick and needed care. Dr. Hall, the prison surgeon, brought some of the men to my home." Sarah's gaze shifted downwards, and she spoke softly. "I tended to them until they were in good enough health to return inside the stockade. Everyone I helped made it back, except one. He was a young boy, Hugh Berry, and he died in my arms. I couldn't bear for him to be buried in that unmarked mass grave, so I put him to rest in my garden."

"That was a kind thing to do, Mrs. Johnson." Harry's mind raced. "Did you say there was a mass grave?"

"By October, so many men were dying every day that the commandant ordered mass burials. It's a sight I won't ever forget, not as long as I live. Every afternoon at two o'clock a wagon came through those gates loaded with the dead. Took them to an abandoned cornfield and buried them together. There's near eighteen long trenches now in that field. They called it the 'dead house.'"

"What became of the other prisoners?"

"Like I said, in February they were all transferred out. Those who were the most able-bodied marched to Greensboro and then on to Wilmington. The sick were taken to Richmond."

"Then why the fire? Did folks in town burn the prison down?"

Sarah's face grew grim, and a hint of anger flashed across her face. "After the prisoners were all gone, this was nothing but a supply depot. Then just a few days ago, a Union officer, General George Stoneman, marched into Salisbury. Said he was here to free the Federals now that General Lee had surrendered. But they were all gone, and he ordered his men to set the prison on fire to remove any trace of what happened here."

"At least no one was harmed by his actions," said Harry. His questions had been answered, he thought, except one. "Ma'am, is there anyone who might have a list of the prisoners who died, and those who were transferred?"

"Looking for your friend? I nearly forgot in telling the story," she said. "The commandant is gone, as are his men. May I ask your friend's name?"

"Josh Ricker. From Maine."

Sarah let out a gasp; the back of her hand brushed against her lips. "He stayed at my house while I tended to his fever. Such a small, sweet boy. He got better and I had to send him back, give his bed to another." Hesitantly, she turned away from Harry and stared at the distant fields.

"Ma'am?"

"He's out there," Sarah said haltingly, "just over the ridge. Buried with the rest, sir." She turned slowly and looked into his eyes. "I'm very sorry, Mr. Warren. I inquired as to Josh's health a few weeks after he was back inside. I reckon he was just too weak to gain back his full strength, and with so little food—"

Harry pursed his lips, took a sideways glance, and placed both hands on his hips.

"He knew the war was coming to a close, and I remember him crying out in the night one time. Said that someone was coming for him. I thought it was just the fever talking. Now I'm thinking maybe he knew it would be you."

Harry could only shake his head. "I wish it was Josh that was buried in your garden. I wanted to bring him home." Harry looked back at the two horses chewing contentedly on the lush grasses. "I'd like to see the burial site if you don't mind pointing me in the right direction, ma'am."

"My garden is full of flowers, Mr. Warren. Let me cut you a bouquet. You can leave them at the site."

The pain that rippled through Harry dulled briefly as he watched Sarah meander lovingly through her garden, taking great care to select each flower, passing by some with a slight shake of her head, stopping suddenly to cut another. She had remembered Josh, and in her own way, he reckoned, Sarah wanted to show that she had cared.

She walked with him to the ridge, and when they reached its crest, Harry gazed down at the heart-rending rows of trenches, the overturned earth still naked and unmarked. Unlike Fredericksburg, the grasses had yet to reclaim the land and hide the stains of war.

Sarah handed Harry the flowers and took a step backwards. Offering her a slight smile in return, he tipped his cap, turned and started down the ridge, his footsteps as heavy as his heart.

"Long, long afterward, in an oak
I found the arrow, still unbroken;
And the song, from beginning to end,
I found again in the heart of a friend."
—Henry Wadsworth Longfellow, *The Arrow and the Song*

CHAPTER 15

Elijah picked up the cracked and weathered stools in his father's cabin, carried them out the door, and set them on the dusty ground. Unlike April in Maine, the evening air, warm and comfortable, was as familiar to Elijah as his own skin. He thought of earlier times, how slaves often toiled in the fields well past sundown, hungry, bodies aching from the backbreaking work. Now in the early hours of evening, he sat on a stool, his belly full of boiled chicken and greens, dumplings laden with broth.

As Pappy emerged from the cabin, Elijah studied him, aware that years of unrelenting labor had taken its toll on his father. With his stooped shoulders and deeply lined skin, Pappy looked much older than his mid-fifties Elijah knew him to be. Settling onto a stool, Pappy lit his corncob pipe and took a long, first puff. Content to listen to the crickets chirrup in the fields, father and son occasionally stole a glance at each other, smiled, and for a while, let their easy silence speak.

Finally Pappy snuffed out his pipe and tapped it against his knee. "After you run off, Fowler came here tearin' up the pea patch, hollering for his money. Mastuh Ramsey, though, he talk that Fowler down, say you don't skedaddle without no reason."

"Elijah whipped most every day."

"Mastuh Fowler brung Ol' Joe with him. He come find me. Tell me what Buckra done to you."

"Ol' Joe? You meet Ol' Joe?"

"He tell me about your back." Pappy put his hand on Elijah's arm. "Show me what they done."

Elijah lowered his head. As much as he hated to show his scarred back, this was his father, and he knew he had a long story to tell him. He stood, unbuttoned his shirt. Slipping it off his shoulders, he tucked it in around his waist.

Pappy placed his hand on Elijah's arm, turned him around, and then ran his hand over his bumpy, ridged back. Tears welled in the back of his eyes.

Long, jagged scars ran up and down Elijah's spine, disappearing below the band of his trousers.

"Lord-a-mighty, my boy. How this ever heal? Skin all tight."

"Ol' Joe, he say Buckra gone kill Elijah soon enough. So he tell Elijah to run. Just like you say, Pappy, run like the wind."

"Tell Pappy all, son."

Well into the evening, Elijah retold his story. Pappy occasionally shook his head in disbelief, but asked few questions. It was enough to sit beside his son and listen to his voice.

Finally, his eyes rimmed red, his father interrupted. "You be going back to Maine?"

Elijah hung his head. "Yes, suh. Maybe you come with Elijah?"

Pappy relit his pipe. Leaning his elbows on his knees, he stared into the growing darkness. "After I hear we was all freed, went right off to your mama's grave. Told her we ain't slaves no more. Remember all them blue violets out there?"

"Yes, suh."

"They's sprouting up all around her. She always loved them blue violets." Pappy took a long puff on his pipe. "Listen to them crickets out there making all that racket."

"Pappy?"

"Ain't leaving your mama, son."

"But Elijah make this promise."

"Pappy feelin' too old now. Only thing I knows is them fields out yonder."

A lithe figure emerged from the darkness.

"Pappy Sol? Who you talking to?"

She moved with the grace of a swan, her dark, expressive eyes catching the fire's light. Then her hands flew to her face; her mouth opened in stunned surprise.

"Elijah? That you?"

"Talitha!"

"Lord have mercy! I been praying you was alive, that you'd come back."

He tried to stand; thought his knees would give out and sat back down. The girl he had kissed in the cornfield had grown into a beautiful woman. Words locked in his throat; he couldn't even make his tongue work.

"Anytime, Elijah, you can get yourself off that stool and give this girl a hug."

In his awkwardness, Elijah finally stood, knocked over the stool and shyly moved toward her. His arms reached out for her. He pulled her close. Felt her heart beating against his chest.

"Elijah, ain't you got nothing to say?" Talitha laughed as she leaned her head back and looked into his eyes.

"You is more beautiful than a spring morning."

"Oh, Elijah." She trembled.

"Talitha been takin' good care of me. Don't leave Pappy be, no suh, she always tryin' to do the cookin'. Don't think a man can wash his own clothes."

"Don't you be fussing about me, Pappy Sol." She picked at his soiled shirt and brushed flecks of dirt from the sleeve. "Ain't never seen no one come off them fields with more dirt on his clothes than you. You'll be hollering for me soon enough."

For a moment Elijah felt as if he had never left. The late nights sitting around the fire, the playfulness between Pappy and Talitha unchanged. Even as a child she had been adoring of his father, watching out for him over the years. He stared lovingly at her and could only smile.

When Pappy at last stood and stretched his aching limbs, Talitha ushered him off to his cabin, planting a kiss on his forehead.

"You gets your rest, Pappy Sol. You mind if Elijah and me goes for walk?"

"Mmm-hmm. Pappy Sol knows about the cornfield."

He lost all sense of time and place, as if the missing years had eclipsed under the moon's yellow light spilling over the fields. He thought it had been enough, to see his father, to feel whole again, and yet the rush of emotion he felt when he saw Talitha unnerved him.

"Cornstalks was over our heads—right out there—when you first kissed me," Talitha laughed. "I was wanting more than one kiss back then."

"Mastuh, he close by in the field when we kiss."

"When Mastuh sold you, it all happen so fast. You was just gone. I'd lie awake at night, thinking about that kiss. Us slaves don't cotton many memories. Good ones, that is. Least I had me one."

"Elijah never forget."

Talitha spoke softly. "Maybe I can have me that kiss now? I've been waiting a right long time."

This time he did not hesitate. He turned to face her, and taking her chin in his hand, he raised her lips to his as she pressed her body against him, her arms around his neck.

"I never told you, Elijah. Don't know why, especially since my heart was all afire."

"Tell Elijah what?"

"I fell in loves with you right then in the cornfield. After we kiss."

"Elijah din know, din know."

"All this time. Wondering, hoping to hear some word where you be. When Pappy Sol tell me that you run, I knew you'd make it. So I been waiting, and now you home."

"Talitha—"

Talitha kissed him lightly on his lips and then pressed her finger over his mouth. "You think on what I say. Tomorrow you tell me all. Ain't much left of this night, and the only thing I want right now is you."

"For some cause or other, the slaves, no matter how often they were repulsed by their masters, were ever disposed to regard them with less abhorrence than the overseer."
—Frederick Douglass, *The Autobiography of Frederick Douglass*, p. 53

CHAPTER 16

"**W**here's Digger?" hollered Buckra as he watched Caleb move timidly into the barn. "And where's the horses?" He stacked the last bag of feed onto the pile and then reached for his half-filled bottle of whiskey.

"Th—thieves," stammered Caleb, biting down on his lower lip.

"What thieves?" Buckra set the bottle down on an overturned barrel, grabbed Caleb under his arms and slammed his back against the barn's center post. Caleb felt his lungs pressing against the inside of his ribs.

"Thieves? Tell me everything or I'll break every bone in your body."

"Fella told me to tell you they was thieves. But they killed Digger. Took the horses, our rifles." Caleb grimaced at the foul breath spewing from Buckra's wet lips. "We was at the Danville station, you know, looking for runaways like you told us. Digger got plum excited when he spotted someone. Said he looked familiar, like maybe he had been one of Fowler's slaves who'd run off a long time ago. He was with a white fella."

"Go on," Buckra said, easing his hold as he reached once more for the whiskey. This time he threw back his head and took a long swig. Caleb blew out his breath but he dared not move.

"They was walking, headed south out of town, and Digger, he said we was going to follow them. By the time we got our horses, they was already gone from sight. Figured they took off into the woods and was following the road."

"Hmm. Trying to hide," mumbled Buckra.

"Digger said we'd catch them as long as they didn't know we was tracking them." Caleb told him that after two days, there was still no sight of them, not even a campfire. "Digger had some kind of feeling about this here slave. He was like fleas on a dog about him. Said the fellas would surface soon enough or make a mistake, and then on the third night we finally spotted a campfire in the woods, not far from the road. We come at them just before dawn."

"So you two goons, with loaded muskets, sneak up on them while they was sleeping and somehow Digger dies, you live and lose the horses?" Buckra hacked in disgust; spat a wad of spittle onto the hay. "Can't wait to hear the rest of this."

Caleb described how they had moved in quickly, and that Digger had placed his hand over the darkie's mouth and pinned him down with his knees. "I tied his wrists while Digger kept him quiet." Then Digger, he said, walked over to the white boy and woke him, pushed his musket into his chest. "Things went wrong when Digger sent me to get the horses." He related how when he came back, Digger was out cold on the ground, the two standing over him, Digger's musket in the white fella's hand.

"I leveled my rifle right at them, but then everything happened so fast. Digger come to, and when I looked down at him, the darkie went and tackled me, knocked the rifle out of my hands. Digger grabbed it and aimed it at the white fella, but he got off the first shot and struck Digger right in the chest."

"Blasted idiots. And he let you live?"

"The white fella said he wasn't wanting to kill either of us. Just happened, is all."

Buckra took another long swig.

"You said Digger thought the slave looked familiar? You get a name?"

Sweat trickled down Caleb's furrowed brow. "I don't remember. But I think he might have known you."

Buckra seized Caleb again, twisted the collar of his jacket and pulled him close to his face. "Then you'd better think real hard. I need a name."

Caleb took a deep, trembling breath, and struggled to remember. "I-I don't know—Ezra maybe. Or Efron—Eli—Elijah. Elijah! That's it."

Buckra rocked back on his heels, released his grip. "I'll be danged—he's alive," he said, more to himself than to Caleb.

Buckra was finished with his frightened hire; his mind plotting at a feverish pace. "Git out of here," he said, "there'll be no money for you. If I ever see your face again I'll shoot you myself." He barely noticed Caleb racing out into the night.

After drinking the last of the whiskey, Buckra tossed the emptied bottle into the hay. His thoughts rushed back to the day Fowler arrived at the plantation with the young slave. With his broad shoulders and muscled arms, the slave's whole bearing had frightened him.

Buckra staggered to a three-legged stool. He had always offset his rail-thin body by instilling fear in others. The only way he knew to handle the powerfully built slave was to break him, like a wild horse. He remembered that first night, how he had forced Elijah with his whip to eat from a trough while hungry pigs grunted their displeasure. He had lashed Elijah twice the next day for no reason other than to instill fear. Elijah's back had frozen in pain, and he had to crawl his way back to the cabin. Buckra chuckled. He remembered telling Fowler the slave was defiant, and had refused to work the fields.

After three tortuous months, Elijah had escaped, and Buckra still longed for revenge.

"I need to wake Ol' Joe, the miserable old coot," he muttered. Shaking his head from his whiskey-induced headache, he stood and walked unsteadily out the barn.

Ol' Joe slept soundly on his plank bed under the warm comfort of his wool blanket. He had spent his entire life at the Fowler plantation and, in spite of his new freedom, he had chosen to live out his last few years in the one-room cabin that had been the only home he had ever known. Fowler had always watched over the elderly slave, and no one, not even Buckra, had ever dared to touch him. In the short time Elijah had been at the plantation, Ol' Joe had cared for him as if he were his son, tended to his raw-whipped back in an effort to save his life. Finally, knowing that Buckra had planned to do Elijah even more harm, possibly even kill him, he had told Elijah to run. To follow the North Star.

Ol' Joe felt someone shaking him awake. Rubbing the sleep from his eyes, he stared in confusion as Buckra stood over him, his whiskey breath fouling the air.

"I want you ready to leave before dawn."

"Where I going, suh?" Ol' Joe asked.

"We're taking a ride, you and me."

"Where to, suh?"

"Ramsey farm—near Salisbury. I need you to show me the way since you been there with Fowler."

"Why we going there, suh?"

"I've unfinished business with Elijah."

"Elijah there? He alive?" Ol' Joe sat upright, shaking his head. "Please, suh, ain't no need to hurt the boy. He a free man now. Let him be."

Buckra struck Ol' Joe across the face with the back of his hand.

"Don't push me, old man."

Recoiling from the stinging blow, Ol' Joe ran his bony fingers over his swelling cheek.

"We need to leave before anyone knows we're gone. I'll be back for you in a few hours time."

Ol' Joe lay trembling, fear consuming him like an unexpected storm.

"In most of us colored folks was the great desire to able to read and write. We took advantage of every opportunity to educate ourselves. The greater part of the plantation owners were very harsh if we were caught trying to learn to write… Our ignorance was the great hold the South had on us."
—Project Gutenberg, *Interview with Mr. John W. Fields*, ex-slave

CHAPTER 17
May, 1865

Shafts of sunlight streaked through the paned windows, scattering the afternoon light on the wall of books that faced Oren Cheney's tidy walnut desk. The shelves ran the length of the room, holding his most treasured collections. Although Oren had been home in Lewiston a week, the events in Richmond, the news of President Lincoln's assassination, and the arduous task of fundraising had taken its toll on him. As a fire blazed in the small hearth, Oren's favorite clock, which sat squarely on the mantle, chimed softly to announce the hour. His office was a great comfort to him, and turning his face to the window, he gazed out at the campus green. He relished such moments of solitude, and on rare occasions allowed himself to feel a sense of accomplishment as he watched students pass near his window.

While he tried to focus on the work to be done, the thousands of dollars still needing to be raised, his tired thoughts all too easily drifted to more pleasant recollections: his delightful seat companions John Laird and young Jamie on the train ride home. Oren had been charmed by the twelve-year-old and his determination to take on the task of schooling Elijah. Oren smiled to himself, and then reflected on the group of former slaves on the streets of Richmond, who, like Elijah, had never penned a single line across a sheet of paper or experienced the wonder of reading a classic well into the night. Indeed, he realized, education was the real challenge for what was now several generations of a single race, most of whom had been deprived the simple basics of learning. "Just as I have been concerned for the young people scattered throughout Maine without a means to education," he said out loud, "we must find a way to educate this race." Nearly four million former slaves had suddenly been thrust into a new world of independence and self-reliance without training or education. "How do we rebuild not only a nation, but also a people? What is to be done with, and for, the colored people? How will they use their freedom? Who will educate them?" He ran the questions through his mind with an overwhelming sense of responsibility.

He entertained the thought recruiting a few former slaves who, by fortune of his or her circumstance, may have had enough schooling to succeed at Bates. This would be a discussion he would look forward to with his board of trustees. Picking up his quill pen, Oren made a note to himself to take up the matter with Ebenezer Knowlton, the trustees' chair, in time to raise it at their next meeting. He was confident that with the trustees' approval, he would figure out a way to recruit a few capable candidates.

Hearing a knock at his office door, Oren reluctantly pushed his thoughts aside. No doubt Fidelia, his cherished assistant, would quickly bring him back to the many tasks at hand.

"Come in."

Three former students, David Cobb, Edward Frye, and Charles White, who had attended the school when it was the Maine State Seminary, entered the office, wide smiles across their faces.

Their unannounced visit delighted Oren, and after much greeting and catching up on their activities, he inquired as to their unexpected call.

"The three of us are deeply concerned as to the plight of the freed slaves. Their brain and hand have been untrained, and we feel a deep obligation to see them gain a proper education," began David Cobb. "We longed for their emancipation, and we now feel in some ways responsible."

"And a growing concern of mine. In fact, I was pondering it right before you arrived," said Oren.

David Cobb smiled. "That does not surprise us, which is why we came to see you and seek your counsel. We've come with a plan."

"Such as? I'm already intrigued."

"We're going to Virginia, to look at sites to establish schools for the colored people."

"And do you have any locations in mind where this would be possible?"

"Brother Brackett is already teaching at Harper's Ferry in West Virginia, where there is government land and facilities, and the location is a beautiful one, between the Potomac and Shenandoah Rivers," said Charles Webster.

"We'll be looking at other locations, mostly in Virginia to start," added Edward Frye, "but we are eager to hear your opinion on our idea."

Steepling his fingers, Oren gazed momentarily at the hearth. "When I was in Richmond recently, I happened upon a group of freedmen on the street. I asked them what plans they had for the future. They were quick to point out the overwhelming challenges they faced. These men were a mix of ages, both young and old, and I believe not one could read or write. I had nothing to give them but God's word."

"I'm sure there was comfort in your words."

"Perhaps. Yet I see more clearly now that I have more to give to this race than I previously thought. Education is of the highest priority, and with my ability to raise money for such a purpose, and the political connections I've garnered over the years, we could help make things possible."

"Then we have your blessing that ours is a worthy plan?" said Cobb.

"No question, however great the challenge. An old friend of mine, Reverend Cowell, came to me one day when I was ministering in Lebanon and offered me a lot of land and $100 to build an academy. A considerable challenge for me at the time. I did not hesitate then, nor would I do any less now for the colored race. But my first thought is that like Lebanon Academy, the schools you build should be Freewill. Solomon tells us in Proverbs that 'Wisdom is the principal thing; therefore get wisdom; and with all thy getting get understanding.' You asked for my counsel, and I feel that the spiritual side, the wisdom, will be as important in these schools you wish to establish as is the getting—the understanding, the learning. They must go hand in hand."

In silence, the three men nodded in agreement.

"If you are to tackle this deed, you must be assured, first of all, that it is God's will. Good works flow from our faith as James reminds us in the Scriptures. But as to this great deed you pursue, can any real faith be shown to exist without a life of good works?"

"Yet the task before us is so great."

Oren moved from behind his desk and sat on its edge in an effort to be closer to his former students. "'Whatsoever thy hand findeth to do, do with thy might.' You have before you a cause that is worthy and just. You are young and full of energy and spirit. Go forth with your good works and do it with all your best."

Oren bowed his head. "Let us commit this task to prayer."

"What you are to do without me I cannot imagine."
—George Bernard Shaw, *Pygmalion*

CHAPTER 18

Shoulders sagging, Harry stirred restlessly in his saddle as he headed down the road to the Ramsey farm. His horse, as if mirroring his master's mood, trod slowly. Elijah's horse, tethered to the saddle horn, whinnied in the still air, his tail swishing at flies.

Elijah heard the whinnying, looked up from where he kneeled along the tilled rows, and saw Harry. Then he saw the second horse, the empty saddle. He shook his head, and calling out to Harry, he stood, picked up his seed bag, and headed out to greet him.

"Harry, suh," said Elijah, wiping the sweat dripping from his brow. "No Josh?"

Grimacing, Harry shook his head. "All I can tell you is that he's buried in what used to be a cornfield."

"Cornfield, suh?"

"Yeah, along with hundreds of others. Maybe thousands, if anyone's counting. All them prisoners who died, just buried in one big ol' grave." Harry dismounted, brushed the dust and dirt from his jacket, and began walking beside Elijah.

Elijah took in a long breath. "Preacher say we all in this here struggle, but we finds our reward in Heaven. Maybe Josh up there shouting and a-singing with the angels now. Maybe he with Billy, suh and this Leighton."

"Hope you're right about that." Harry looked out over the endless rows of overturned earth. Backs arched under the late afternoon sun, both coloreds and whites painstakingly worked their way down the furrows, dropping seeds from their bags and patting the readied soil with the backs of their hoes. "What're you planting out there?"

"Them fields all corn." Pointing his arm to a more distant clearing, Elijah said, "Over there, them fields been fallowed for a time. Wheat be planted 'cross the way. Workers over there got sacks full of animal dung."

"Wouldn't want that job. Leastways, planting's going on here. We'll be lucky if the lilacs are blooming by the time we get back home."

Elijah sensed Talitha's presence. His back stiffened.

"Back home? What this white folk saying, Elijah?" She appeared beside him, her voice gripped with fear. Resting her seed bag on the ground, she placed her hands on her narrow hips and stared long and hard at him.

"Talitha—" Elijah sputtered, "this be Harry, suh; he—"

Harry stared at the striking woman. Strands of dark copper hair curled beneath a blue cotton head-wrap framing her angular face. Beads of sweat, like tiny pearls, glistened on her light brown skin.

"Ma'am," he said, touching his cap. "Name's Harry Warren."

Crossing her arms around her chest, Talitha's eyes narrowed to slits, offering only defiance.

"Right pleased to meet you," he said in an effort to fill the awkward silence.

Paying him no heed, Talitha turned to Elijah. She studied his face, his eyes, searching for assurance, a nod, anything to dismiss the white folk's talk of home.

Unable to meet her gaze, Elijah lowered his head. "Talitha, this no time." Timidly, he reached for her hand, but Talitha brushed it aside, leaned over, and grabbed her seed bag.

"I'll see you after sundown," she said, her voice barely a whisper. "You knows where I'll be." Without a backward glance, she turned and bristled away.

Elijah watched her leave, his gaze never wavering until she disappeared across the fields.

"I'm thinking you've a decision to make," said Harry, breaking the silence. "Not an easy one."

"Decision all made," Elijah answered as he untied the reins of his horse from the saddle horn. "Elijah go with you."

"You all right with that?"

"No, suh."

"Guess neither one of us is feeling good right now."

Harry stepped through the door of the small cabin that was Pappy's home, a one-room structure with a wooden chimney and dirt floor. Sparsely furnished, the kitchen consisted of a small, dark table, a three-legged stool, an iron pot and a hand mill for grinding corn. He looked around for a bed, saw only a plank against the wall. A basket of dried corn shucks was tucked in the corner.

Harry was quick to reach for Pappy's hand. The man received it shyly, and gestured for Harry to sit down on the single stool.

"Say, it's a right fine evening," said Harry. "Let's the three of us move outside. It feels like a summer evening in Maine to me," he said with a laugh to soften the awkwardness he felt.

Elijah gathered another stool from the cabin next door and set it on the ground. Pappy lit his corncob pipe, took in a long puff, and watched the smoke curl against the evening light. "Come sundown, coloreds sit down like white folk do. No more work them fields with the moon over our heads. We just be free. President Lincoln give us that. He deliver us, and now he gone."

No one spoke, silence their only requiem.

The quiet lingered as they sat and watched a bank of clouds settle over the fields. A dog barked in the distance.

Finally, Pappy began to talk. "Corn crop all made for the year."

"How's this farm going to be managed now?" asked Harry, eager for conversation.

"Mastuh Ramsey, he tell us coloreds we free to leave the farm. Some do, like Silas. He waiting for them Yankees give him his own piece of land. Right off, Mastuh say if we stay on and work he give us a wage soon enough." Pappy puffed on his pipe, looked out at the freshly planted rows and said, "Now he say white folk talking about sharecropping."

"What this sharecropping, Pappy?"

"Croppers is coloreds and poor white folk. Mastuh Ramsey, he go and give plots of land to croppers. He buy the seed, the fertilizer, all them tools we use. Come harvest time, each cropper give Mastuh half his yield."

Harry became intrigued. "So then you'll own a plot of land?"

"No, suh. Just work it."

"How much land for every cropper?"

"All depend. Mastuh Ramsey, he got one thousand acres or more. He say maybe us croppers get fifty acres apiece. Maybe one hundred if more coloreds leave."

Elijah leaped from his stool. "Pappy, you don't be tending no fifty, no one hundred acres by yourself. Ain't even got no mule. How you go and farm this land? "

"Lord take care of me, boy."

"No, suh, Elijah needing to take care of you," he shouted, "and this croppers' land you go and get." Elijah paced back and forth, kicked loose dirt with his boots, turned and paced again.

Harry lowered his head. Pappy tapped his pipe against his knee. A pall settled over them like a dark, misty shroud.

"Ever has it been that love knows not its own depth until the hour of separation."
—Kahlil Gibran

CHAPTER 19

Pappy slept fitfully on his plank bed. Quietly Elijah moved past him, opened the door, and stepped into the night. Harry, although awake, lay still on the ground just outside the cabin, his saddle for a pillow. Content to make his bed beneath the stars, he watched in silence as Elijah moved through the darkness.

Elijah headed across the fields to a stand of trees. He knew Talitha would be at its edge, waiting for him under the willow oak. It was here, under its sprawling branches, that Elijah gathered on Sundays with other slaves to hear the preacher, an elderly slave who had learned to read the Bible during his years of servitude in the Ramsey household. On his run north with Billy, Elijah remembered entering a church for the first time and seeing Billy's surprise that he had never been inside one before. Confused, Billy had asked why slaves didn't have a church to hear the word of God. Elijah responded that they did, under a willow oak. "Lord hear us just the same," he had answered.

It was on those ephemeral Sunday mornings that Elijah and Talitha became friends. Barely out of childhood, they had filled their eager hearts with hope from the preacher's words. Then, in the spring of his sixteenth year, Elijah was sold, shattering their dreams. During the past few years, believing he would never see her again, Elijah had convinced himself that Talitha had been merely a childhood friend and nothing more. He could not bring himself to look deeper into his heart. Until he saw her again. And in that instance, he knew that separation would be almost impossible to bear.

His heart tormented him as he walked through the meadow, fragrant with wildflowers. How could he leave Pappy and now Talitha again? Then the old, familiar images flashed over and over in his mind. Billy. Missus Johanna and Missus Anna, Quakers, who had risked their own lives to see him safely on his way to Canada. And William Still in Philadelphia, who said Billy earned a badge of honor from the colored folk for saving Elijah. Honor. And a solemn promise. His mind repeated the words over and over. He could do no more, no less, for one small boy, Jamie.

Elijah knew he had no right to ask Talitha to wait. She was beautiful, eager for love, and free. Already she had endured enough pain for one so young. Her lighter skin was testament to that. She came to Mastuh Ramsey's when she was four years old. The owner of a neighboring tobacco plantation, a handsome man of sixty, had fathered her. His younger wife, embarrassed by his indiscretion, could not bear the sight of the child. Master Ramsey's wife willingly received her, passing the responsibility of raising the child to Tempie, their cook, a full-bodied older woman who embraced her. Shy, uncertain of her place, Talitha hugged the coarse cotton of her new mother's long, white apron, and rarely strayed from the warmth of the large farm kitchen. For five years she blossomed in the security and constancy of Tempie's love. But then Tempie collapsed on the kitchen floor. Too young to assume any of her adopted mother's household duties, the grieving nine-year-old child was sent to the fields.

Talitha stood under the tree, leaning her back against its wide trunk. Elijah breathed deeply when he gazed upon her. He looked at her willowy body, her round dark eyes, and her full lips. Only their eyes spoke. And then he came to her, tenderly pulling her into his arms.

For a long while neither said anything.

Finally Elijah opened his mouth to speak, his throat suddenly dry. He cupped his large hands in hers. "Elijah got something to tell you, Talitha."

She stepped away from him, wrapping her arms around her thin shoulders. Her voice edged with fear. "When I walked away from you today, I went to see Pappy Sol. He tell me there's a white boy got you all tied up. Tell me about the child."

Elijah reached for her, placed his arms around her waist and then lowered her onto the grass. He started from the beginning and, leaving nothing out, he told her of his escape, his run with Billy, Canada, and then finally Maine and the boy. "Jamie, suh, he a good boy. He like a bird with a broken wing when Billy, suh die," he said in a low tone. "Then he ask Elijah to take Billy's place, be his big brother. If Elijah don't go back, other wing go and break, and Jamie, suh, he ain't never go and fly again."

Her eyes flashed anger. "He a white boy! You think white folk do you the same?"

"Some do, Talitha, some do."

"You don't owe white folk nothing!"

Elijah kept still. When he didn't respond, Talitha asked in a softer voice, "What about us?" Her eyes held tears. "All this time I been thinking you feel the same way about me."

"Elijah love you, Talitha," he interrupted. "But it ain't right asking you to wait, even if it be just for a time. Elijah know his heart. This where he belong."

"Then stay, oh Lordy, please stay." Raising her small arms, she pounded a fisted hand onto his chest before she collapsed against him. "No, Elijah, you can't leave me."

He looked up at the fading stars, the moon sinking over the distant hills. Anywhere but her lovely face. If only he could stop the dawn from stirring, hold on to this small moment. If only he never had to let her go.

*"As I would not be a slave, so I would not be a master. This
expresses my idea of democracy."*
—Abraham Lincoln

CHAPTER 20

In the clammy pre-dawn dark Buckra rolled up his blanket and tried
to shake the dust and dirt from his jacket and pants, but the morning
dew had flattened the grime against his clothes like a thin coat of
smeared mud. He was angry with himself. Late yesterday he had been less
than a mile from the Ramsey farm and had planned to confront Elijah by
sundown; instead, he had fallen into a drunken stupor and was forced to
sleep it off. Ol' Joe had surprised him, pulling a bottle of whiskey from his
saddle pack and baiting him to drink. Buckra had purposely not brought
any whiskey with him, but the sight of the amber-colored liquid was too
great a temptation. Promising himself only one long swig to steady his
nerves, he had hungrily grabbed the bottle. One drink had all too easily
turned into another, and Buckra soon knew he had lost his battle for the
night.

He nudged Ol' Joe awake, and with his knife cut the rope he had
bound around the old man's wrists as he had each night, lest he should
try and escape and alert Elijah.

Ol' Joe lay on his back rubbing his aching wrists, relieved to at least
feel the blood flowing again, all the while desperately trying to think
of another way to stall for time. Yesterday he had tempted Buckra with
whiskey, knowing Buckra would easily succumb. Throughout their
journey, he had kept the bottle hidden in his saddle pack, and had pulled
it out only when they were perilously close to the Ramsey farm. He knew
Buckra would not resist, but for his plan to work, he had counted on

Buckra forgetting to tie his wrists, his mind muddled from liquor. While Buckra slept, he had hoped to steal his revolver that rested on the ground beside him, and race for the Ramsey farm. Yet in spite of his drunkenness, Buckra had bound his hands before passing out into a bottomless sleep.

"Time to go, old man."

"Need a moment to get the blood flowing. Fingers still numb."

"Jest git on your feet."

With a heavy sigh, Ol' Joe tossed his blanket and made his preparations to leave.

"You try anything this morning, I'll shoot you." Buckra checked his gun, a Colt New Army Model he had purchased from a wounded soldier who was on his way home, and, satisfied the ammunition chamber was full, untied and mounted his horse. "Take me straight to his pa's cabin. You call Elijah out—tell him it's you."

As they walked their horses out of the woods and onto the road, Buckra scanned the early morning sky, pleased that the sun was only but a faint yellow line along the eastern horizon.

Ol' Joe said nothing, his head lowered as if to deny the day and all that was about to unfold. He knew no other way to stop Buckra. All was in God's hands. As the horse plodded along, he offered a desperate prayer.

The road soon opened to an expanse of fields, and in the distance, he spotted the Ramsey farm, its stillness interrupted only by the customary stirring of a rooster crowing at the dawn. Ol' Joe had no choice but to lead Buckra to the long row of slave quarters behind the barn, halting just before a cabin beside a sprawling oak.

In spite of the early morning shadows, Buckra saw a man lying on the ground not far from the fire pit, his head resting on a saddle. "White man," Buckra whispered to himself. "Got to be the fella who killed Digger."

Suddenly the white man's eyes flashed opened. Startled, he quickly rolled on his side and reached for his rifle.

The hammer cocked on Buckra's pistol. "Don't touch that rifle. Git up and keep your hands where I can see 'em." When he felt satisfied that the man was no longer a threat, he said to Ol' Joe in a low tone, "Call for him."

"Please, suh. Don't make me do this."

"Call him or I'll shoot this white boy."

Ol' Joe wiped his chin with the back of his hand. "Elijah! It's Ol' Joe." Moments passed. The door creaked open.

Wearing only his trousers, Elijah rubbed the blurriness from his eyes. Since his painful good-bye with Talitha less than two hours ago, he had slept fitfully on the cabin floor. He stared through the semi-darkness at the figures on horses. And then his whole body shook. "Oh Lord, no, no," he stammered.

Buckra smirked. "Long time, Elijah. Long time."

"I tried to find a way to stop him, my boy," cried Ol' Joe.

"Shut your mouth, old man."

Elijah stole a glance at Harry, standing ram-rod straight, his hands resting on his hips, his rifle on the ground.

"Reckon your friend here killed my hired hand. That's Digger's musket. I'll deal with him after I've squared with you."

Behind Elijah, his face raw with fear, Solomon tried to pull his son back from the doorway. Instead, Elijah quickly moved to block his father. "Harry, suh, you go inside. This my fight."

"I ain't moving a rat's inch," responded Harry.

"No, he ain't," added Buckra. "Get off your horse, Ol' Joe. Elijah's going with me." A sneer wormed his face; his eyes filled with menace as he ran his free hand over the whip tied to his saddle. "If you're still alive by the time I finish with you, I might just do you a favor and shoot you. Put you out of your misery as if you was a wounded dog."

As Ol' Joe dismounted, he tried to thrust his body at Buckra's horse, hoping to knock the gun from Buckra's hand, but the overseer kicked him in the face, sending him sprawling onto the ground. "Get the rope and tie Elijah's wrists."

A lone silhouette suddenly stepped out from behind the oak, his shotgun leveled at Buckra.

"Lower your gun, Buckra, and toss it aside."

"Mastuh Fowler!" Ol' Joe struggled to his feet, and with the back of his hand wiped blood from his lips. "You done get here after all."

His revolver still pointed at Elijah, Buckra shook his head in confusion. "What in daylight?"

Cautiously Fowler moved forward. "Elijah's not going anywhere with you. Now put the gun down."

Buckra gritted his teeth, but held his gun steady. "I'll be danged.

Finishing the job for you, is all. He run off—you lost money on this slave."

Fowler stared long and hard at his overseer. "I should have fired you years ago."

He took a cautious step forward and said to Buckra, "Ol' Joe tried to warn me after you left his cabin, but I was gone—business in Durham. The missus told me all. Ol' Joe said to tell me he would try to stall for time, let me catch up. As it was, I had to take the train. Only just got here myself."

Fowler stole a glance at Elijah. "My fault that I believed the things Buckra said about you. Too late for me to change what happened, but I won't let him harm you again. Make no mistake, Elijah, I know I was hard on my slaves. Fact is, I've been hard on lots of folks. And that time in the curing barn? Buckra hoisted you naked on a rope, whipped you, and rubbed your back raw with a dried corncob? He said you had refused to plow. So I let him have his way with you."

Elijah shook and lowered his head. "Elijah plowed the fields good, suh."

"After you ran off, Ol' Joe set me straight about that. I may not be the nicest man around, but I don't cotton outright murder." He took a long, deep breath. "And I'm sorry for what happened."

Still aiming his shotgun, Fowler took another step closer. "I don't want to shoot you, Buckra. So toss your gun down. Let's end this now. I'll give you what I owe you and then some. But I want you gone."

"I've waited too long for this." Buckra spat onto the ground. "I'll leave the white fella be, but Elijah's coming with me. Best not try and stop me."

"Enough. This is my last warning. Put the gun down and get out of here."

"I've worked for you for ten years, Fowler. This time you're in my way."

Buckra whipped his revolver around, aimed at Fowler and pulled the trigger.

Fowler's shotgun exploded.

The sharp crack of gunfire shattered the dawn. The frightened horses reared; Buckra toppled to the ground. Ol' Joe scrambled out of the way as hooves glazed near his head. Harry rushed into the fury, intent on grabbing Buckra's revolver. He shouted to Elijah, "The reins, grab the reins!" But the horses fled.

Then he saw Elijah dropping to the ground and pulling Fowler into his arms. "I gets them," Solomon shouted to no one in particular as he chased the terrified horses across the fields.

Harry stood over Buckra, who lay motionless. Fowler's shot had not missed; blood congealed around Buckra's chest, no longer flowing. He knew Buckra was dead, yet instinctively he bent down and felt for a pulse. Nothing. He took a deep breath, picked up the revolver and tucked it into the back of his trousers.

Blood spewed from Fowler's shoulder. Ol' Joe unbuttoned his shirt and hurriedly tried to find a spot less stained with sweat and grime. "Got no choice," he muttered as he pressed the soiled cotton firmly onto Fowler's gaping wound.

He didn't know if Fowler could hear him, but Elijah cradled his former master in his arms, unable to let him go. "Hang on, suh, you just hang on," he whispered over and over again. Harry dropped down on his knees and yanked off his rope belt.

"We need to get mastuh to a doctor, suh."

"He's losing blood too fast, Ol' Joe. We've no time." He tied his rope belt tightly above the wound. Then lifted the bloodied shirt from Ol' Joe's hands and examined the ripped open flesh, saw that the bullet had not passed through.

"I've seen enough bullets taken out. I'll have to do it." He looked at Ol' Joe and said, "Make a fire, if you will. Elijah and me are going to take him inside."

"Yes, suh. Here come Solomon with the horses. He all tuckered out."

Harry shot a glance at Elijah's father. "If you'd boil some water, please. And we need some clean cloth."

"Yes, suh," he said, gasping for air. "Solomon tie up the horses, boil the water, and git you some clean cotton. Yes, suh."

Early in the evening, Fowler opened his eyes to a dazzling sunset streaming through the window. Never had the fiery red sky appeared so radiant to him. He turned his head, aware that he was in Solomon's one-room cabin; he saw him and Ol' Joe, and the young white fella—Harry? And there was Elijah with a beautiful young woman sitting on stools around the small kitchen table. A kettle of soup rested in its center and the scent of biscuits wafted across the room.

"Buckra?" he asked, his voice weak and trembling. Heads turned in his direction.

Pushing back his stool, Harry walked over and stood beside the makeshift bed. "He's dead, sir. We put his body in Ramsey's wagon. Ramsey said he'd take care of things."

Fowler nodded, blinked tears from his eyes and stared vacantly at the ceiling for several long moments. He attempted to move, winced as pain pulsated through him.

"Try not to move your shoulder and arm just yet, sir. Ramsey said he would bring the doc back. Reckon you're going to need some laudanum for the pain."

"The bullet?"

"It's out, sir."

Fowler stared knowingly into Harry's eyes. "You were a soldier."

"Corporal, 17th Maine. Not exactly on your side of things."

"I've made my mistakes, young man."

"Not today, sir."

Fowler offered him a slight smile and gazed again at the lowering sun, its brilliance fading beneath the window ledge.

"You want some soup, suh?" Solomon asked, breaking the silence.

"I'd like that." Fowler tried to shift his weight as if to lessen the pain. "You could use a mattress atop this plank, Solomon."

Solomon grinned. "Be in your own bed soon enough."

At last Fowler's eyes, dark and somber, met Elijah's. "I had to do this."

Elijah took a long, deep breath. "Thank you, suh. We good, suh, we good."

From the diary of Oren B. Cheney:
"Come to John Storer's. Write out a plan for a freedmen's college."
—Emeline Cheney, *The Story of the Life and Work of Oren B. Cheney*

CHAPTER 21

The handsome four-story building across the street from the city hall was one of Dover's taller structures. Three dormers emerged through the high Mansard roof, and between the imposing eight-paned windows separating the second and third floors stretched a sign that ran the length of the building: Freewill Baptist Printing Establishment. The New Hampshire city had been the headquarters of the newspaper *The Morning Star* since 1833. The weekly was first published in Limerick, Maine, in 1826 and later moved to Dover, which was deemed a more central location. Since its inception, the popular paper had concerned itself mainly with religious content. It did not involve itself in the anti-slavery movement until 1834, when William Burr became its editor and publisher. Burr viewed the institution of slavery as a moral and religious issue and immediately used his new position to radicalize the paper, launching a rigorous campaign against the evils of slavery. It had been a bold decision by Burr, as many patrons felt the weekly should not delve into social issues. His unrelenting stance nearly ruined the newspaper financially, as protests called for a more moderate position on the issue of slavery. Finally, in 1837, the paper's board of trustees voted to continue the anti-slavery campaign, an audacious commitment that continued throughout the antebellum years. As a frequent contributor to *The Morning Star*, Oren took advantage of the paper to decry slavery, writing, "We can find no language that has the power to express the hatred we have towards so vile and so wicked an institution. We hate it. We abhor it. We loathe it. We detest and despise it as a giant sin against God, and an awful crime upon man."

Remnants of a fine morning mist rising over the Cocheco River evaporated in the warming sun as Oren made his way across the busy Dover street to see his old friend William Burr. As he opened the door, a bell jingled faintly, announcing his arrival. Printing presses clacked loudly from the back of the room, and in the forefront shelves ran the length of the building's walls, stacked with yellowed copies of the newspaper's decades of printed history.

William Burr glanced up from his cluttered desk, his dark eyes full of purpose. His brown hair framed his high forehead and strands of gray streaked his chinstrap beard. Leaping to his feet, Burr offered Oren a warm embrace and ushered him to a worn leather armchair. He closed his office door and sat down next to Oren, bypassing the seat behind his desk. Respecting each other's valued time, the two men rarely spent any time exchanging small pleasantries.

"A delightful surprise! No doubt another visit to a potential donor, my friend?"

With a heavy sigh, Oren nodded. "The task of fundraising for the college was arduous," he said, and finally admitted he was reeling under the strain. "My trustees have given approval for six months of vacation, but I must forgo any rest at this crucial time. Investors in Boston have pledged fifty thousand dollars on condition that within three years, I am able to secure one hundred thousand dollars. And separate from that, I must raise an additional thirty thousand to secure the state appropriation of land."

Burr was astounded by the staggering amount of money Oren was driven to raise, but nevertheless, in his typically calm and deliberate manner, strongly urged him to take an extended rest.

"*I am willing to cut off years from my life, if I can see the institution established on a firm foundation,*" Oren responded. "Well, my friend, this all reminds me that I must make haste to Sanford to meet with another donor, John Storer. Perhaps I can secure another thousand from this most generous man."

Making his goodbye, Oren hurried his way to the station. The train carried him over the Salmon Falls River, swollen with snowmelt, into western Maine and through large tracts of fertile farmland. From his window, he spotted infant buds opening in the warmth of the May sun, tender green against the stark white birches. Like the Virginia spring he witnessed just weeks ago, a sense of renewal once again filled his soul.

Storer welcomed Cheney into his home, a grand mansion that stood in testament to his success. He'd begun humbly as a clerk in a store in Kennebunk, and later owning a variety of his own businesses. In his retirement, Storer, known for his kind and generous nature, indulged in many philanthropic ventures. Oren had made the visit to ask for $1,000 for the college, but before he presented his request, Storer excitedly told him of a large gift he was contemplating. "I should like to give ten thousand dollars to an organized body I trust could manage it and add to it. *My thought is to make this gift a permanent blessing to the colored race.*"

Immediately, Oren saw a unique opportunity for the school in Harper's Ferry and quickly pushed his own interest aside. "John, hear me out. Some of my former students, all involved with the Freewill Baptist Home Mission Society, came to see me recently. They are already at work with the Freedmen's Bureau to establish schools in the South. I also became aware that Reverend Nathan Brackett has already established a primary school in one of the war-torn buildings at Harper's Ferry, West Virginia, and is teaching reading, writing, and arithmetic to freed slaves."

"How did that come to be?" asked Storer.

"Brackett served as chaplain during the war and came to know Harper's Ferry. He saw hundreds of colored people living in tents with little hope and little to live on. There are over thirty thousand freed slaves in West Virginia alone. Brackett has requested more missionary teachers, and we need more schools. *"Why not give the money to the Free Baptists? They have always been true to the colored race."*

Storer rose from his chair and stood in the front of the granite fireplace. Turning to Oren he said, "*I should like to give it to your people, for I honor them for the position they have taken, but I fear they are not financially strong enough to carry on and develop such an enterprise, as it should be managed.*"

While Oren greatly respected Storer's sound, discriminating judgment, he remained undaunted, and argued his support for the school.

Finally Storer said, "I'll make this gift of ten thousand dollars, but the Free Baptists must raise an equal amount in one year's time. Let my gift inspire others to give for such a purpose. And if you are successful in raising the matching funds, then I believe this school will be successful as well."

They talked well into the evening, and by midnight the tenets of a final agreement were reached. The school, they agreed, would teach the primary grades as well as trades necessary for the freed slaves to succeed, but it would ultimately become a college, Storer College. Both agreed that the college would be open to anyone without regard to sex, race, or religion. Oren set a date to meet with Storer again and to present him with a written plan, a task he was only too eager to undertake.

Oren lay in the guest room's four-posted bed, exhausted yet pleased with the evening's successful conclusion. The lantern cast a soft patina as Oren tried to still his mind, but he could not settle his joy over the prospect of a school for colored people. He found himself thinking of the freed slaves on the streets of Richmond and then of Elijah, and wondered if he had found his father. Berwick was not far away, and he made an instant decision that when he returned to see Storer to finalize the plans, he would take a side trip to the Laird farm and share with Elijah the good news of a school not far from his homeland and his father. His tired mind at last demanded rest and, turning out the lantern, Oren pulled the heavy duvet over his shoulders and drifted into a dreamless sleep.

"Help your brother's boat across and your own will reach the shore."
—Hindu Proverb

CHAPTER 22
Late May, 1865

"You're home!" Jamie bounded down the dusty lane and catching his breath, threw his arms around Elijah. "I knew you'd come home, I knew."

In spite of his own heartache, softened by the warmth of Jamie's embrace, Elijah realized he was happy to see him. "Jamie, suh, you gone and growed taller since Elijah been gone."

"You thinkin'? Only been a few weeks, is all."

"You like a seedling. Shooting up come springtime," he teased.

"Maybe I'll be as tall as Billy was." Jamie broke away, picked up a stone, and, taking aim at an old oak, hurled the stone into the air. "Dang, missed. Hey, did you find your pa?"

Elijah's smile wilted, and turning his face away, he watched a hawk circle higher and higher in a thermal spiral until it became only a dark speck in the sky. Finally he said, "Pappy all fine. Now Elijah know."

"Did Harry find Josh?"

"No, he buried with other soldiers down there."

"Oh ... that makes me sad, about Josh. But I'm happy about your pa," he quickly added. Jamie scrunched up his nose. "How can I feel happy and sad all at the same time?"

An ache stabbed Elijah from deep within, Jamie's question mirroring his own. "Sometime that just the way it be."

"Yeah, feels funny somehow." Scanning the distance to the house, Jamie said, "I'll race you the rest of the way."

Flushed and out of breath, Elijah and Jamie entered the kitchen, which was fragrant with the smell of bread fresh. For a moment it felt as if he had never left, the home's familiar sights and smells the only real comfort he had known in the turbulent years of his life. Even Mistah John gave him a firm embrace, and when the missus saw him she cried openly.

At supper, he talked about his father, taking great care not to mention Talitha. He tried to offer assurances that Pappy was doing well and that in time, he would see him again, and perhaps return for a longer visit. Jamie was quick to express his interest in going with him. Throughout the meal, Elijah felt Martha studying him, and although she said little, her eyes asked a thousand questions. Later in the evening, when Jamie settled in with his school work, Elijah stepped outside and leaned against the porch railing. As he stared broodingly at the moonlit sky, he thought longingly of Talitha.

Lost in his bittersweet memories, he did not see Martha come up beside him.

"Thank you, Elijah, for all that you told us tonight. I know it's what my son needed to hear."

"Yes, Missus Martha. Elijah know."

"I see it in your eyes, hear it in your voice. You're torn, if you will, about where you want to be."

Elijah chose silence for his answer.

Wrapping her arm around his waist, Martha said, "Why did you come back? Silly me, I asked a question I already know the answer to."

"This my promise to Billy, suh."

Tears welled in the corners of her eyes. "I hope you stay. It feels selfish to want you to stay, even though I consider you a part of our family."

Elijah turned and looked deep into Martha's watery eyes. "Elijah stay here, Missus. No matter what happen, Jamie, suh, he my brother now. Slave chillun never gots the chance to grow up like chillun should. There pain around them all the time. Most don't get to the other side and see happy."

"And you want that for my son."

"Yes, ma'am. Jamie, suh he still feel pain from his brother's death. Elijah want him to get to the other side. See happy. This make life better when he all growed. Then Elijah go."

"Elijah was a man with a nature like ours."
—James 5:17

CHAPTER 23

Shards of dawn sprinkled the morning sky as Oren hurried down the porch steps, enthused over his success with John Storer the previous night. After reading the agreement Oren had meticulously prepared over the past two weeks, Storer took his quill pen, and by his signature committed ten thousand dollars for the school in Harper's Ferry. Having begged off breakfast, Oren made his way to the Sanford train station, reminding himself that he had a good friend in Berwick who no doubt would lend him his wagon to make the short trip to the Laird farm.

By mid-morning, Oren steered the horse up the winding lane. An austere clapboard farmhouse loomed in front of him, and a lilac bush as high as the eaves spilled its pale blossoms on the weathered porch like droplets of rain. A large but simple hay barn settled naturally on the lower slope as if it had always been a part of the land.

John Laird stepped from the barn door, furrowed his brow and then smiled in recognition. "Reverend," he said, hastily raking his fingers through his hair and slapping bits of straw from his pants. Harry Warren poked his head around the barn door. As Oren climbed down from the wagon, John took hold of the horse's reins and secured them around a fence post. "Harry, grab that bucket over there and get some water for the horse."

Harry dipped the bucket in the trough next to the barn and set it down in front of the horse. "Nice to see you again, sir, ah, Reverend."

"And you, Harry. Appreciate the water. I'm sure this old horse is thirsty after climbing Pine Hill." Oren turned his gaze to the rolling fields around him, the occasional birches pock-marking the stands of pine and hardwoods. "A nice place you have here, John, and so close to the river."

"We've not a lot of land, but we work it hard and it sustains us."

"Mister John works it better than most. Folks in town all say it," added Harry. "I got me some land with my wages from the war, and will be farming soon enough, but I've been dogging him to learn how he does it so well."

"What brings you our way, Reverend?" asked John.

"Had a business meeting, another fundraising venture, in Sanford, the result of which might be of interest to Elijah."

"Whatever might that—"

"Reverend, suh!" Elijah appeared at the fence gate, handsome in red flannel, his shirttail hanging loosely over his dark blue trousers. His eyes widened with curiosity. As he opened the gate, he leaned a long stick against a post. "Them cows is all out in the back meadow now, Mistah John." Oren observed an easy, unspoken union between the two men; John closing the gate behind Elijah, and then gently tugging at his shirt. Grinning in understanding, Elijah struggled to tuck the shirttail into his pants.

Oren beamed. "Wonderful to see you again, Elijah" he said, "I wasn't sure if you and Harry here had yet returned from the South." Elijah immediately stiffened at the remark; a flicker of sadness passed over his face. Oren caught the subtle movements. It must be about his father, he worried.

"Let's all make our way to the house. I'm sure there's a warm blueberry pie. Saw the missus carrying jars from the pantry earlier," said John.

"I'm needing to get home," said Harry. "Be back in the morning, sir." He turned and shook Oren's hand. "Nice seeing you, Reverend."

"We'll go over the planting times then, Harry," said John with a nod of his head.

Oren held back until Elijah walked beside him. "Did you find your father?"

"Yes, suh."

"Is he in good health?

"He all right."

"And still at the same farm?"

"Pappy, he stay on there." Elijah went on to explain how many of the freed slaves had begun working under a system of sharecropping, and that he expected his father to have nearly one hundred acres of his own to farm.

"Is he farming this land alone?"

Elijah lowered his head and said nothing, scraping his muddied boots across the porch as reason for his silence. Oren did not repeat his question.

After introducing Oren to Martha, John shuffled and gathered chairs around the table. Opening the cupboard, Martha reached for the top shelf. Behind a stack of white porcelain dishes, she carefully withdrew a single cup and saucer of delicate bone china patterned with pink and yellow rosebuds. It was the only piece of fine china she owned, a gift from her mother on her twelfth birthday. She set the cup and saucer in front of the Reverend and placed three white mugs on the table. Moving a vase of lilacs to the side, she poured the boiled coffee.

"I don't know which smells sweeter," said Oren, "the lilacs or the blueberry pie."

"I'll take the pie," smiled John, clasping his hands around his mug.

"Lilacs, the harbinger of spring," said Oren. "To each season something is notable; the roses of summer—"

"The black flies of spring," added John.

"God has a sense of humor," retorted Oren. Both men fetched a grin.

When Martha served the pieces of her pie, Oren offered a short blessing. Conversation flowed easily; twenty minutes later Martha gathered the empty plates, placed them in the sink, and returned to the table. "Jamie will not be pleased to have missed your visit," Martha said. "But he does enjoy his schooling."

"Tell me again—how much, if any, schooling have you had, son?" asked Oren, turning his attention to Elijah.

Martha grinned. "I guess that depends on what you call schooling, Reverend."

"Oh, yes, I do recall now. Young Jamie. Principal and teacher."

"Reverend, you said earlier you may have some news that would be of interest to Elijah," said John.

"And the purpose of my visit today." Turning his face to Elijah, he said, "Like you, there are freed slaves who never had the opportunity to learn to read or write. I believe, as do others, that our country has an obligation to educate your people, both men and women. Right now, there are Freewill Baptists who are working in the South to establish schools for such a purpose. I know of one primary school already under way in Harper's Ferry, and I had a thought that if you had found your father, Elijah, you could be closer to him, and attend this school. I would be happy to take care of your travel to make this happen." Oren paused and said in a soft tone, "What I am saying, Elijah, is that you can go home."

Silence filled the room. The Lairds glanced at each other, their eyes expressing anguish at the unexpected turn in what had been delightful conversation. Elijah stirred uneasily in his chair, his gaze fixed to the floor trying to hide the well of emotions coursing through him.

"Elijah has a home here," said John, breaking the uncomfortable stillness.

Martha stared at Oren, her voice choked with sobs. "This is all so, so fast. And Jamie, he's so attached, he—"

"I'm plum unprepared for this discussion, Reverend. I'll go no further with it." John pushed back his chair from the table. "We'll leave you be with Elijah. In the end, it's his choice to make," he added, casting a glance at Elijah.

Oren's hands trembled and he placed his cup on the table. "Please, forgive me. I was so focused on what I thought was a good plan, my enthusiasm got in front of me. Apparently, I did not think this through."

"Good day, Reverend," John said sharply. "Martha." Taking her arm, he led his wife from the room.

"I have grievously erred. It's very clear this family considers you one of their own, Elijah."

"Yes, suh. Elijah, too." Shoulders slumped, Elijah played nervously with his fingers. Taking a gulp of air, he asked meekly, "So this be a school for us coloreds?"

"Yes, it will also be open to men and women of all religions, and all races, but I suspect the school will fill its seats mostly with former slaves."

"And it be free?"

"Yes."

Elijah bit down on his lower lip. "Elijah can't go, Reverend, suh."

"Tell me more, please."

"Elijah promise Billy, suh. No white folk ever do for Elijah what he done." Elijah explained his promise, and how when Billy died, Jamie withdrew from everyone, closeted in his own silent world. "Like he in there hiding hisself from his pain. First time he talk again, it be to Elijah. Me and Billy be like brothers, so Jamie, suh, he want that too." He let out a sigh. "This promise Elijah keep."

"Hmmm … I didn't realize how fragile the boy—" Oren stopped himself in mid-sentence.

Elijah stirred and got up from the table. "Coming in here, you ask about Pappy. He too old to work all them acres by hisself." He hesitated, paced the floor, turned and paced again. "And, and then there be—"

"Someone else, Elijah?"

"Yes, suh. Talitha."

"Do the Lairds know about Talitha?"

"No, suh. Ain't gone tell them." Elijah sat down, his head in his hands.

"I've only added to everyone's distress," Oren said as he leaned across the table and touched Elijah's hand. "But I'm seeing things more clearly now; I'm reminded of a story in the Bible. May I tell it to you?"

"What this story about, Reverend, suh?"

"The prophet Elijah."

"There be a prophet with Elijah's name?"

Nodding, Oren began. "Elijah was a man of God, and he was sent to Ahab, king of Israel, to tell him there would be years of drought because he and his wife Jezebel had done evil in the eyes of the Lord, not unlike your slave owner and his overseer. Then God told Elijah to flee Israel and hide by the brook Cherith, east of the River Jordan. God directed the ravens to give Elijah bread and meat, and told him to drink from the brook so that he might live." Oren leaned forward, resting his elbows on the table. "Was there not someone who fed you by the water, so that you might live, Elijah?"

"Billy, suh! He give me food by the creek. Elijah hide there from the slave catchers." Rapt with curiosity, Elijah stirred in his seat. "What this prophet go and do then?"

"Sometime later the brook dried up because there was no rain, so God told Elijah to go to Zarephath, a city in the west, and there he would meet a widow who would give him food. So Elijah went to Zarephath and met the widow while she was gathering sticks outside the city's gate."

"Don't know no Zarephath, Reverend, suh," interrupted Elijah, furrowing his brow.

Oren smiled. "The city is not important, my son. But what follows is. Elijah asked the widow for some water and a piece of bread. She told him that she had no bread, only a handful of flour in a jar and a jug with very little oil, and that she needed to make enough bread for herself and her son to eat. But Elijah told the widow to make him a loaf of bread first, promising her that God would not let her flour be used up nor her oil run dry until the day the rains came to bless the land."

"How that be?" asked Elijah.

"It was the word of God, spoken through Elijah. God was testing the widow's faith, but she complied. Thereafter, Elijah, the widow, and her son always had enough bread to eat. Then one day the widow's son, the young boy, became very ill. He grew worse and worse, and finally he stopped breathing."

"This boy go and die?"

"Yes, but Elijah cried out to the Lord and asked that the boy be returned to life. God heard Elijah's voice, and the prophet held the boy until his soul again entered his body." Oren paused and reached again for Elijah's trembling hands. "Do you see, my son? God gave Elijah his life, by the brook, and in return, Elijah gave life to another—the boy."

"Yes, suh," Elijah said, his voice choked with emotion. "This all mean Elijah don't let Jamie, suh die. Elijah hold him, Reverend, suh, hold him and don't let go." He wiped the tears welling in his eyes.

"This how the story end?"

"About the boy in the Bible, yes. But your story does not have to end with just the boy. I believe we can find a way to give you a life beyond as well."

"How we go and do that?"

"Right now, I need to pray and to ask God for guidance, my son."

"You think someday God let Elijah be with Pappy and Talitha?"

"All things are possible with God."

"You think God even let Elijah go to school down there?"

"What school? Down where?" Jamie stood in the doorway. Unbridled fear sat on his face. His schoolbag crashed to the floor.

"Why are you taking him from me?" He screamed, turned and ran up the stairs.

"Elijah needing to take care of this."

Nodding his agreement, Oren pushed away from the table and made his goodbye.

He was distraught as he untied the horse and drove the wagon down the lane. The Laird family was in shambles and it distressed him greatly to know that he had not served any one of them well. A deepening sense of responsibility to make things right pervaded his being. "The story will not end here, Elijah," Oren promised.

He looked out across the pasturelands without seeing them. "I must be prosperous, Luther. And today I failed you."

From the diary of Oren B. Cheney:
"Ask Congress for all of Camp Hill and take what you can get."
—Emeline Cheney, *The Story of the Life and Work of Oren B. Cheney*

CHAPTER 24

Over the next two weeks Oren busied himself with matters of the college. At the meeting of the trustees, he brought forth his plan to recruit a small number, perhaps six to eight, former slaves. Most of the college's trustees had been staunch abolitionists, so his proposal, as predicted, was easily accepted.

Before the end of the meeting, Oren told the trustees he desired a short break from his collegiate duties, and soon thereafter he set out for West Virginia to meet with Reverend Nathan Brackett. He had written to Nathan the terms of Storer's gift, and following Nathan's approval, they had made plans to seek the most appropriate site for the proposed college. Nathan, his wife, Annie Dudley, and Oren toured three possible sites in northern Virginia, and in the end, agreed the most desirable location remained Camp Hill in Harper's Ferry, a breathtaking spot at the confluence of the Potomac and Shenandoah rivers. All the land and buildings, which had served as the U.S. Armory and Rifle Works during the war, was still government owned, and here, working under a lease, Reverend Brackett currently operated his primary school in Camp Hill's Lockwood House, the former paymaster's quarters.

Oren was delighted to learn that a bill had been introduced in the Senate providing for the sale of all government buildings and land that remained at Harper's Ferry, and that in one section of the bill, certain churches and schools currently under lease would each be gifted a single lot of land. Suddenly he had another thought.

"Nathan, we need more than a single lot of land for a college. I'm thinking we should ask Congress for all of Camp Hill, which will be several more lots of land, and take what we can get."

The following day Oren and Nathan descended on Washington, calling on the two Maine senators, William Fessenden and Lot Morrill, who Oren had known and conducted business with during his short political life as a state senator.

"Senator Fessenden, if I may." Holding the bill in his hand, Oren took off his spectacles, rubbed his eyes and put the glasses back on again. "You just told us that this bill goes before the Military Committee today. I'm reading here that the Secretary of War conveys only a single lot of land for Storer College. It is quite fortuitous that you're a member of this committee. Is there any way that you could amend this bill so that we could ask for more?"

Fessenden shrugged his shoulders. "I could ask the committee's chair for more time to examine and to amend the bill. If he agrees, he'll not give me much time, perhaps only a few hours, but we can certainly try."

"Then Nathan and I will be close at hand," said Oren, pleased with the response.

Fessenden ran his hand along his chin, paused, and said, "Wait for me in my hotel room."

Oren and Nathan paced anxiously in the senator's room. Finally Fessenden appeared, and with his approval, they quickly amended the section of the bill to include four lots of land, constituting seven acres of land and four government buildings for Storer College.

"This is as far as we can take our efforts," said Oren and he handed the amended bill back to the senator. "The land for Storer College remains in the committee's hands. And the will of God."

Tired, yet feeling a great sense of triumph that he'd at last had a hand in establishing a school to help raise the colored race, Oren made preparations for his departure home.

"This is your college, Brother Brackett. We have many of our fellow Freewills eager to help you as you go forward. As for me, I will work to secure the matching funds. Then I must step back and return my energies to Bates."

As the train pulled out of the Washington station, Oren leaned his head against the back of the seat and tried to rest. Yet something niggled in the back of his mind, refusing him sleep. Something about the proposed

Reconstruction Act before Congress that would allow the emancipated slaves to work their way up and out of the labor class by distributing land confiscated or abandoned during the war. He tapped his fingers against his brow as if willing his tired mind to think. Could something like this work for Elijah? Provide him a way out of his dilemma? By the time Washington and its environs vanished from his view he collapsed into an exhausted sleep.

"There is no flock, however watched and tended
But one dead lamb is there!
There is no fireside, howsoe'er defended,
But has one vacant chair!"
—Henry Wadsworth Longfellow, *By the Fireside*

CHAPTER 25

Talitha stared at the firelight, tears welling in the corner of her eyes. She sniffed, blew her nose, and stuffed the square of ragged cotton in her apron pocket as Pappy stepped out from his cabin. "You needing anything else, Pappy Sol?"

With a shake of his head and a slight chuckle, Pappy grabbed a stool and sat down beside her. "I fine. You go on now. Get yourself some rest. Only be a few hours afore you fussing over me again."

"Just because Elijah done left me ain't no reason for me to stops watching out for you."

"Child, I told you I don't believe Elijah left you."

"Then where he be?" Talitha's eyes flashed with anger. "Buckra's dead. Elijah ain't got to fear him no more; got no reason to run, and still he go."

Pappy sighed. "We been all through this. Every night. I knows it hard." Pappy leaned his elbows on his knees and stared at the dying embers. "My boy, Talitha, he just like me."

"How you mean?"

"He only gone love one woman." Pappy turned to her with a small smile.

Talitha shrugged her shoulders. "Hmmpf. You didn't leave your woman to take care of some white child."

Pulling his pipe from his pocket, Pappy tapped it against his knee, letting the fine ash fall to the ground. "Never had to run off from the mastuh like my boy did, neither. Then this Billy, some white folk he don't even know, go and save his life. Reckon even I'd see things different after that." He took a long pause. "Elijah doing what he think be right."

He knew his words offered little comfort, and for a long while neither spoke. It hurt him to see her brood, night after night, staring into the darkness half hoping, half expecting Elijah to reappear. After the confrontation with Buckra, Elijah and Harry had stayed two more days until Fowler felt he was able enough to travel. Overjoyed that his plan to stop Buckra had succeeded, and grateful to his former master, Ol' Joe had been eager to take Fowler home. On the morning of Elijah's departure, Solomon had given his son his blessings, but had also admonished him not to neglect his own chance to rebuild his life as a free man. Although Talitha had been at Elijah's side since the incident with Buckra, she was not there when Elijah and Harry had mounted their horses to leave.

"Here come that fool Jackson," said Pappy, looking up from the fire, puffing on his pipe. He watched the tall, handsome man strut pompously toward them. "Most like he lookin' for you again."

"I knows." Talitha lowered her gaze, stirred nervously on her stool.

"Walk like he own you."

"Well, he don't." Her eyes fixed on the fire, her voice a near whisper, she said, "He not so bad, Pappy Sol."

"Mmm-hmm."

"At least he here." Talitha straightened her shoulders and pushed a ringlet of hair away from her brow. "You hush up, now, Pappy Sol."

"Been looking for you, Talitha." Jackson searched for another stool, and finding one, set it down beside her.

"I here with Pappy Sol."

"How you doin', Solomon?" Jackson asked, with a nod to Talitha.

"All right."

"How much land Ramsey go and give you to farm?"

"Ain't said." Pappy stiffened, and then crossed his leg over his other knee, his foot swinging slightly in the air.

"Understand Elijah come back after all this time."

Pappy only nodded.

"Hear he went and took right off." Jackson stared into the fire, letting his words hang pointedly in the air. "Nothing to hold him here is what I'm thinking."

"Didn't know you ever done much of that." Pappy relit his pipe.

"Pappy Sol!"

Pappy glanced at Talitha and, sensing her unease, turned back to Jackson. "Elijah's got him some business up north. He back soon enough."

"Maybe. Maybe not." Jackson tried to reach for Talitha's hand, but she pulled away. "Way I see it, some things don't wait. Not when you care about folk."

"Jackson, don't—"

"Seems like he's turned his back on his people."

"I ain't hearing no more of this!" Leaping to her feet, Talitha fled from the fire's light.

Jackson called out to her. "You knows where I'll be." With a short nod to Solomon, he stood and walked away.

Solomon kicked Jackson's stool, glowering as it tumbled across the yard.

From the diary of Oren B. Cheney:
*"What does Cheney want now? Oh, he is trying to build
another railroad to the moon."*
—Emeline Cheney, *The Story of the Life and Work of Oren B. Cheney*

CHAPTER 26
June, 1865

Three weeks after Oren's return from Washington, he traveled to Northwood to attend the New Hampshire Yearly Meeting of Freewill Baptists, a meeting regarded as one of the denomination's most important gatherings. Early in their establishment, the Freewill churches throughout northern New England organized themselves around a number of regional quarterly meetings as a means to come together and discuss denominational business. From these meetings, representatives were selected to attend and make reports at the all-important Yearly Meeting.

The town of Northwood ran along the old turnpike road, its long main street fronted with taverns to accommodate the sledges and stagecoaches passing between Portsmouth and Concord. The Freewill Baptist meeting house sat on Clark's Hill, a gentle slope near the center of town. Arriving early, Oren sought out the Yearly's presiding officer. He asked for, and received, permission to address his colleagues following their collective reports, sharing with them the plans for a proposed college in Harper's Ferry. He would ask his colleagues for their support in helping him raise funds to match John Storer's ten thousand dollar pledge, a request that would doubtless cause a great deal of debate and discussion. Sweat tricked between the folds of his shirt, which he attributed more to his anxious nerves than to the unaccustomed humid June air.

As church representatives and other attendees gathered and mingled before the call to order, word quietly spread throughout the room that

Oren was on to another new venture.

"Elder Cheney has asked to address the meeting," said Silas Finney.

"What does he want this time?" Thomas Deacon shook his head.

"Surely it is not of such importance that he addresses the meeting," said Henry Gilman, one of the younger ministers. "He's just one member among many."

Deacon laughed. "Obviously you do not know the man."

"I've heard him preach a time or two. I must admit, he has a certain way about him," offered Finney.

William Hurlin, who had been standing nearby, overheard the discussion and moved readily into the group. "After what I observed in Richmond two months ago, I heartily agree that Oren has a certain way about him. We visited the Confederate prisoners held at Libby Prison, and Oren spoke to them. At first they seemed not to want to hear from a Yankee preacher, but once Oren began, it was not long before most went down on bended knee. The men were without hope, filled with despair. Our good brother gave them a path back to God."

"It only confirms that Oren would not be asking to address us if it were a matter of little consequence," said Deacon, turning to Gilman.

"What do you mean?" said Gilman.

Finney said, "Our denomination has many fine men, men of vision. But in this generation Brother Cheney has no equal.

"Oren has a way of getting things done, of that you can be sure."

"Then what could he be addressing us about? Has he not enough to deal with?"

"What does he want now?"

Finney shook his head and threw up his hands, "*Oh, he is trying to build another railroad to the moon.*"

A few hours later Oren was called to the pulpit. Wiping the sweat from his brow, he looked out at the assemblage of curious faces. "Brethren, given the lateness of the day, and my unanticipated request to address you, I will get directly to my reason for being before you. And I promise to keep my remarks brief." He paused as muffled laughter rumbled through the hall.

"During the last year of the war, Brother Nathan Brackett, who I'm pleased to say was an alumnus of the Maine State Seminary, was stationed by the Christian Coalition in the Shenandoah Valley. He saw hundreds of refugees—men, women, and children—who had escaped their slave owners and sought safe haven in Harper's Ferry. In a letter home he wrote, *'We have a colored population huddled together with almost nowhere to live and nothing to live on.'* Brother Brackett has become intimately acquainted with the needs of the colored people, and at the war's end, he set up a primary school in a war-torn building in Harpers Ferry and began teaching them reading, writing, and arithmetic. He also found classroom space for two other schools nearby, and as a representative of the Freewill Home Baptist Mission Society he is directing the efforts of missionary teachers to provide a basic education to former slaves."

Oren noticed several heads nodding. "Allow me to tell you a story, which I must confess, gave rise to the idea I will shortly present. One of Brother Brackett's students, a thirty-year-old former slave, seized his education like no other in the classroom. In a few short weeks, this young man was reading exceptionally well. Apparently he saw his fellow students struggle to learn in spite of our good teacher's tireless efforts. He approached Brother Brackett and asked if he may take the lead with his people. And with a classroom style that cajoled unlike any of us has experienced or practiced, he sparked not only their enthusiasm, but did so in a way that incorporated their culture of learning."

Holding up a letter, Oren continued. "Brother Brackett writes that he is in need of more teachers from here, but perhaps there is a much greater service we can provide." His voice reverberated through the room. Listening intently, the members stirred in their seats, unsure of where Oren was leading them.

"Whatever might that be?" shouted an impatient voice from the back of the room.

"The answer, my friends, comes from the story I just told. Our colored brethren are not less than we are. They do not lack ability, only the tools that we so often take for granted. Once those tools are sharpened and in their hands, there is no limit to what they can do. I believe that we can equip the colored people to teach other coloreds, rather than rely so heavily on missionary teachers. They will learn more from those who have suffered with them. In the faces of their own, they will see the hope of a better future."

"How can we make it happen?" Many in the hall echoed the remark.

Oren took a deep breath. "John Storer, a most kind and philanthropic man from Sanford, one whom many already know, has offered a gift of ten thousand dollars to create a school, ultimately to become a college where coloreds will learn the skills to teach each other."

"The gift is conditional, however," Oren went on to explain. "An equal sum must be raised in one year. Brethren, we cannot in the eyes of God be mere onlookers. We have long held that it was not the will of God that human beings should be held in bondage by their fellow man, and now that the colored people are free, we have a moral obligation to help. Education is the path, and now is our time to act. I ask that you join with me in this most important challenge, to build upon John Storer's gift and raise the necessary matching funds."

A few members spoke out freely, endorsing the movement, but the formidable financial task stirred serious objections from several doubters. Oren met the objections one by one as they arose with deftness and resolve. He also announced that through the efforts of Senator Fessenden, it was anticipated that Congress would convey a lot of land and four buildings for the purposes of establishing a college for emancipated slaves.

"Brethren, this request has nothing to do with me. I believe we have a common purpose in this great effort. Remember that Nathan Brackett is one of our own. And I believe it is the right thing for us to do."

Finally, the Reverend George Ball spoke, his voice booming across the hall over all the others. "*This is a magnificent project, and I will be an earnest worker in helping you carry this out.*"

Feeling more hopeful, Oren relaxed a little and allowed a faint smile. He told his colleagues that John Storer had named the trustees of the fund for the college, which included himself, Nathan Brackett, Ebenezer Knowlton, Silas Curtis, George Day, J. M. Brewster, and George Goodwin.

By the end of the meeting, a temporary "Commission for the Promotion of Education in the South" had been formed. Emotionally exhausted, but feeling a great sense of relief, Oren gathered his coat and headed for the door. Senator Fessenden stood in the front hall, and seeing Oren, hurried to greet him.

"Well done, my friend," he said, "and I'm pleased to see that efforts will be under-way to match John Storer's gift." The senator told Oren the War Committee had voted in favor of the bill to give land and buildings to Storer College as amended, with no discussion, and that it would be moving to the Senate and House for a vote, but he could not offer a time as to when the final vote would be taken.

"These two initiatives, securing the land, and creating a commission to raise the matching funds, are in motion, and we have much to be thankful for," replied Oren. The senator slapped Oren gently on his back and stepped into the warm night air. "I shall be in touch."

"Senator," Oren said, placing his hand on Fessenden's shoulder. "There's another matter I should like to take up with you, if I may have one more moment of your time."

Fessenden smiled and shook his head. "My good Oren, is there no end to your dreams?"

"This is of a more personal nature, but in order to make it happen, if it's possible at all, I would need your help."

"And what help is that, although I'm afraid to ask?"

"I understand there is a great deal of confiscated or abandoned land in the South, and that there are plans afoot to distribute the land to newly freed slaves. That they may become landowners."

The senator sighed. "You are only partly right about that matter, my friend. Our intent in Congress was that all land confiscated by the Union Army was to be distributed to the freed slaves by either the military or the federal Freedmen's Bureau that we established. At the end of May, however, President Johnson announced his own Presidential Reconstruction, and one of the things it called for was that all confiscated lands would revert to its prewar owners."

"Forty acres and a mule," said Oren with a shake of his head. "We owe the colored people that much. Generations of unrequited labor."

"I quite agree, but President Johnson is adamant about state's rights, and it's his view that the southern states had never given up their right to govern themselves. The federal government, he believes, has no right to interfere with questions at the state level."

"Then doubtless few freed slaves will become landowners."

"Most will rent land or work for wages on white-owned plantations." Fessenden buttoned his coat. "What was your interest in this land?"

Oren sighed, his voice wrought with discouragement. "I had what I thought might be a good plan for a friend. Thank you anyway, Senator. It appears I will have to think upon the matter again."

*"Many men go fishing all of their lives without knowing it is
not the fish they are after."*
—Henry David Thoreau

CHAPTER 27
June, 1865

As he drove the cows toward the barn, the sky seemed to Elijah as gray as the granite boulders strewn about the fields. And the cool spring breeze, at once gentle, at once strong, was as unsettled as his spirits. As he closed and latched the fence gate, he wondered if Jamie was home. School would be letting out for the summer, and as a means to celebrate, Jamie had asked that they go trout fishing in the Little River that ran through the woods at the bottom of Cranberry Meadow Road. Elijah had come to love standing on a flattened rock in the shallow of the river, throwing a line and feeling the thrill of a fish strike. Mistah John and Jamie had been his teachers; he allowed himself a tentative smile at the memory of Billy jabbing his sharpened stick over and over in the muddied waters of Goose Creek in northern Virginia. What was it Billy had said? Them fishes all skedaddle. "Billy, suh," he said, chuckling out loud, tapping a fisted hand against his chest.

His mind drifted back to his escape North. Before he had found his way to the fast-moving creek that emptied into the Potomac River, he had stumbled unknowingly into a Confederate encampment, and hiding in the tall grass, perilously close, he overheard soldiers talking about Harper's Ferry, and the battle that led to their successful reclaiming of the strategic town with its military arsenal. Now Reverend Cheney told him Harper's Ferry was the site of a school for colored people. Jamie's efforts had awakened in him a powerful longing to learn, and although he read with difficulty, with each lesson he gained new words, slowly increasing his vocabulary and the ability to read the pages in a book.

Even Missus Martha had spent many an evening with him, guiding him on how to form real words with a pencil in his hand. Elijah was keenly aware that he had been blessed the past two years, but since his visit to his homeland, the longing to be with Pappy and Talitha became a wedge splitting his heart in two pieces, and he could not find a way to make his heart feel whole again.

Hearing his name, Elijah glanced up and saw Harry waving from the barn. He waved back in acknowledgement, and in minutes, Harry was beside him, helping him corral the small herd into their stalls, their bellies laden with milk.

"Been clearing the last of my land," said Harry, "but the sky tells me rain's coming in a few hours, and since the war, I don't hanker being mired in mud again. Thought I'd stop by and see if things quieted down since Reverend Cheney's visit." He had come by the farm the next morning and heard from Mister John that the Reverend, although unintentionally, had shaken the family to its core.

Elijah let out a low whistle. Harry had become a good friend, and he was always pleased to see him. In their trip South, Harry had laid witness to the emotional turmoil looming ever larger inside him. Elijah knew Harry's question was his way of bringing him along, getting him to open up, express his thoughts.

"Most times we talking like nothin' ever happen. Since Mistah Cheney come, Missus Martha, she tear up all the time. She already know it be different. And Jamie, suh, he worry now when Elijah go somewhere. Like maybe Elijah go and run off."

"And Mister John?"

"He don't say much. Most times he all closed up."

"My Mary says Jamie's been right sullen in school. Don't talk hardly at all. Reckon it's his fear. We got to give Jamie more time. He's had to grow up faster than most, but death and separation ain't easy to deal with, particularly at his age. But he'll come around."

"Reverend say he pray this all work out. Maybe God hear him."

Harry couldn't resist a smile. "Well now, Elijah, God listens to all folks. But I'm thinkin' you may be right. Them reverends seem to have a way of jumping to the head of the line."

As they stood in the barn door laughing, they spotted Jamie coming up the lane, his jacket tied around his waist.

"You want any help with the milking before I take off?"

Elijah smiled and shook his head. "Fishes be biting now. Elijah promise Jamie, suh. We do the milking later."

Harry untied his horse, mounted the old mare and headed back to Berwick, waving at Jamie as his horse trotted by.

"Jamie, suh, you ready to go fishin'? Rain coming soon, and we gots to milk them cows when we get back."

"We're really going? Bully!" Full of excitement, Jamie raced up the porch steps. "I'll tell Ma I'm home. Don't you move none."

"Elijah already dig them worms," he shouted after him.

"I'll get the poles."

The short talk with Harry had already lifted Elijah's spirits, and he felt more eager to head for the river. In a cool, dark corner of the barn, he picked up the small worm bucket and whistled at Daisy as he passed by her stall. Daisy tossed her head and whinnied back.

"Where's Ma?" Jamie asked as he raced out of the house.

"Mistah John, he go to town. Maybe she go with him."

"Yeah."

As Jamie waded in and out of the cold waters, Elijah was more content to work his way down the river leaping from boulder to exposed boulder. He stopped when he reached a large, flat rock and studied the current. Just upstream, a logjam had slowed the river to where he stood. Mistah John had told him logs offered the fish protection, and were usually a good place to look for trout. Elijah tossed his line upstream, trying to keep a watchful eye on the worm drifting at its end. Perched on his rock, he found it easy to lose himself in the tranquility of the flowing waters. Glancing over at Jamie, still wading in the shallower water, he smiled at the way the boy chattered to the unseen fish. Not unlike his brother, he thought, when he and Billy had fished at Goose Creek. Jamie, it seemed, was enjoying a piece of his childhood that had been lost to him the past two years. By the time they decided to head home, they had netted three trout.

"Maybe Ma will fix these for supper," said Jamie, staring at the string of trout as they began their way down the trail.

"Elijah cook them fishes one time for Billy, suh when we at the creek."

"Then let's you and me cook 'em right here, like you done with my brother," said Jamie, suddenly stopping.

"We do this come summertime when it be warmer."

"Follow me, Elijah! I want to show you just where we'll make camp." Veering off the worn trail, dodging brush for several hundred feet, Jamie finally stepped in a grassy clearing not much larger than Daisy's stall.

"This here's where I wanted Billy and me to build a hiding place from the army. Figured they couldn't find us, this clearing being so small and all."

"Why din you build this hiding place?"

Lips curled downward. "We was just talking about it when the army came. Never got the chance."

"This hiding place a good spot. Come summertime we cook them fishes right here." Elijah walked over to Jamie and placed his hand on the boy's shoulders. "Billy, suh be with us when we do. He be looking down on Elijah and Jamie."

"I still miss him. Every day seems like."

"Elijah miss him, too. But he at peace now, and he living in here." Elijah gently tapped his finger on Jamie's heart, and on his own. "That mean he never leave us. Now we get ourselves to the barn and milk them cows."

Elijah and Jamie walked the pine-needled forest floor, picked up the trail, and hurried for home as the rain at last made its appearance, falling steadily on their shoulders.

"When trials arise and when danger is near
A light in the darkness I see
This promise so blest bring comfort and rest
The angels have charge over thee"
—Wildie Thayer, Bates College graduate, 1899, *A Hymn*

CHAPTER 28

John Laird paced the barnyard, his anxious strides scattering the brood of hens who hastened an early retreat into their roosting pen. In the distance, thunder cracked open in the darkening sky and in minutes, sheets of rain fell from the laden clouds. He turned to the sound of hurried footsteps, disappointment coloring his face when he saw Jamie and Elijah emerge from behind the barn. Where was his wife?

"You seen Ma?" he shouted at them through the rain.

Racing inside the barn door, Jamie shook the wetness from his hair and held up the string of fish for his pa to see. "We've got trout for supper!" But his father stood outside the door in a silent stare, oblivious to the rain beating down on him. Fear coiled within Jamie like a snake ready to strike. He dropped the fish. "Didn't Ma go to town with you?"

"No, she wasn't with me. I got back some time ago, started milking the cows hoping by then she'd be along. Elijah, when did you last see her?"

"Not since morning time. Then Harry come and we drove the cows into the barn. Never saw Missus Martha."

"Then she's been gone far too long, and her coat's still here." John finally stepped into the barn, shook his head in confusion as he stared at Daisy's stall. The horse lifted her head and neighed. "Wherever she went, she went on foot."

He turned sharply. "Jamie, wait in the house in case your Ma shows up. I'll search the outbuildings, the farmyard. Elijah, search the pastures. I know my wife isn't one to wander beyond her gardens, but we've got to look everywhere. Perhaps she's hurt."

Elijah headed out into the rain-soaked fields. Since the Reverend's visit, he had sensed an almost overwhelming sadness in the missus. By the time he reached the far pasture, it came to him where he might find her.

It wasn't a long walk to Billy's grave, but the rain lashed hard around him, beating on his face and seeping into his eyes. He hurried down the narrow dirt path that wended its way through grassy meadows, at last sweeping left, following the contour of the land as it climbed a gently sloping hill. Lightning flashed and in that instance he saw the crest and the stand of snowy-white birch that surrounded the small clearing where Billy lay. He sprinted through a tangle of underbrush, keeping his sights on the birches bending like ghostly shadows against the rain-whipped wind.

He saw her. In spite of the rain slithering through the tangle of trees, Martha sat on the soggy ground, leaning against the headstone like a broken ragdoll.

Elijah sat down beside her. "Missus Martha?"

Flattened by the rain, a bouquet of Sweet William drooped in her hands.

"Elijah gon take you home now."

She stared at the rain as if it were not there.

"Worry you catch your cold, Missus."

"Stay with me, please." She gazed at the wilted red petals and clutched them to her breast.

"I wanted to bring a handful of Sweet William to lay on the grave. They were Billy's favorite, so I thought—." Her words drifted unfinished. Tilting back her head, she closed her eyes and let the rain fall on her face. "Wish I could cry like the angels are crying now."

"Angels, Missus?"

"The rain. The angels are crying."

"Oh, Missus Martha, Elijah want to take you home. Mistah John, he all worried about you. We go now."

"There's things I need to say."

Resigned, Elijah shook his head. "All right then. You tell Elijah, then we go."

"You remember we spoke some that first night you came back from the South?"

"Yes, ma'am."

"Listening to you, watching you at suppertime, I gathered things were different. Then after Reverend Cheney's visit, I knew things were all coming to a head." She lowered her face and met his eyes.

"Elijah be fine, Missus."

"We both know that's not entirely true. John and I have been unfair to you."

Her words caught him by surprise. "What you mean, Missus?"

She took a deep breath, pushed a hank of wet hair from her face. "When Billy died, my husband and I didn't have a chance to grieve, so frightened we were about Jamie. He withdrew right off, and we were desperate to help him. But he was all locked up inside."

Martha glanced at the small mound of earth in front of her. "It was as if we lost two sons."

She paused, using the silence as if to garner her strength.

Instinctively Elijah knew she would fill the empty space.

Finally her eyes met Elijah's. "We were afraid to speak of Billy in front of Jamie, or show our grief, so worried it would make things worse for him. Mourning for our oldest boy just got bottled up inside for John and me. I felt I couldn't talk to my husband because he had so much guilt about letting him muster. As I said, it was a desperate, desperate time."

"Then Elijah come."

"Yes, then you came. It was like a miracle. Right off Jamie opened up to you. John and I were taken aback by it, yet at the same time so relieved that he started talking again that we shifted our burden of helping him heal onto you."

"It all right."

"No, it wasn't right. I'm sorry, Elijah. We didn't deal with things proper like. And as much as I love you like a son, I've been selfish with you. I knew as long as you stayed with us, that Jamie would be all right. Then when Reverend Cheney told us that you could go home, back to your father and go to school, I was angry with him. Still worried only for Jamie. But I've been doing a lot of thinking, and I know now that Mr. Cheney was right."

Elijah blew out a sigh. He no longer felt the rain seeping onto his shoulders and down his back.

"I only wanted what was best for Jamie." Martha reached for his hand. "It's time I help do what's best for you."

"Elijah ain't leaving now, Missus."

"John and I need to deal with our son. If you could just give me a little more time to talk with my husband and make sure we do this right."

"Missus Martha, Elijah gone tell you a story. Reverend tell this."

He took his time, recalling every detail as he told her of the prophet Elijah. He ended the Biblical tale by saying he now believed he must stay until Jamie was able to let him go.

He saw her body tremble, and he reached for her as she collapsed to the ground as quickly as a thunder clap, her long-held grief set free. He pulled her into his arms, and held her against his chest. "Missus, you go and cry like them angels cry. Only this time it be for Billy, suh. Only one son be gone, Missus. Only one."

He didn't know how long he sat with her, but he was determined to keep her in his arms for as long as she needed him. In the end, he was thankful that he had been the one to have found her. Missus Martha, he thought, had carried her burden alone for far too long.

Finally, her cries quieted, Martha sat up and tried to sweep the wetness from her rain-soaked clothes. She looked up at Elijah and smiled, ran her hand gently down the side of his cheek.

"Thank you, Elijah."

"Elijah take you home now."

She nodded her acceptance, slowly opened her hand, and let the rain wash the Sweet William onto the grave.

The downhill slope flowed with rivulets of mud. Elijah took her hand and did not let it go, even when the rain came to its merciful end, leaving a wake of sunlight on their pathway home.

"In spite of sorrow, loss, and pain,
Our course be onward still;
We sow on Burmah's barren plain,
We reap on Zion's Hill."
—Adoniram Judson, First American Foreign Missionary

CHAPTER 29

It was the first time he had been to Lewiston, and as the train clacked nosily over the bridge announcing its arrival at the Bates Street station, John Laird stared at the great falls, the rush of the Androscoggin River crashing over the pile of jagged rock in its midst. Red brick cotton mills loomed along the river's rugged banks. Leaving the station, John followed the tree-lined street north to Bates College, his anxious nerves churning in his stomach. He had read in yesterday's newspaper that President Cheney was hosting a lecture series at Bates College, which in all likelihood meant that the reverend would be on campus. Armed with that knowledge, John had made an instant decision. It was time to act, to fix what was tearing his family apart, only he just didn't know how to do it.

He wore the clothes he reserved for Sunday worship, hoping to feel less like an uncultured farmer as he made his way to Hathorn Hall. Young men and women rushed past him, laughing and talking with each other with barely a glance in his direction. He followed a group of students up the building's steps and watched them scatter into classrooms as he walked down the hallway until he found the main office, its door wide open.

Fidelia looked up at the tall stranger who stood awkwardly in the doorway. "May I help you, sir?" she asked with a smile, hoping to put the gentleman more at ease.

"Yes, ma'am," answered John. "I was wondering if Reverend Cheney might be about today." He fingered nervously with his hat, willing himself at last to hold it steady by his side.

"Well, sir, he is, but he's with someone right now. Do you wish to wait?"

"Yes ma'am."

"You're welcome to come in and sit down." Fidelia pointed to the two high back chairs straddling her office window.

"Reckon I'll wait out in the hall."

"All right then. Who should I say is calling?"

"John Laird. He'll know me."

"Are you a father of one of our students?"

"No, ma'am, but I got me a boy coming along."

"Then I hope we will see him one day." Fidelia turned her attention back to her desk.

Twenty minutes later, Oren stepped into the hallway and glanced up and down its long corridor, finally spotting John near the front door leaning his back against the wall, his arms crossed in front of him.

"John, delighted to see you. It's good you caught me at this time," said Oren rushing to him, his hand extended. "I'll be at a lecture for the better part of the afternoon."

"I was hoping to speak with you, if you've a moment," John replied.

"Of course," said Oren. "It's a beautiful day. Would you like to walk around the grounds while we talk, or would you prefer to come into my office?"

John shrugged his shoulders. "I'd like to take that walk if you don't mind. Stretch these long legs. I'll be back on the train soon enough."

"We'll head toward the station, then; save you some time. I imagine you'd prefer to be home before dark." Stepping out into the brilliant sunshine, they walked side by side.

"I'm not a talking man, Reverend," began John, "so I'll say right off what's on my mind. Last time I saw you, in my kitchen, I told you I wasn't prepared to hear about Elijah leaving us to go to school down South. I still don't cotton the idea much, but after the war, I knew a day would come when he might choose to move on—"

"Forgive me for interrupting, John, but please allow me to say how sorry I am for the way I handled things. And I had no idea that so much was at stake with regard to your son."

"That's the reason I'm here." John told him of Martha's breakdown, and how Elijah found her at Billy's grave during the rainstorm. His wife, he said, wanted to help Elijah move on, but he remained uncertain as to how to deal with his son if Elijah left the family. "Even after all this time, and all the assurances, Jamie worried that Elijah might not return from the South. While he was gone, there were a few frightening moments when I thought Jamie might slip away from us." Elijah, he confessed, seemed to be the one person who kept Jamie from sliding back into his silent world.

John slowed his stride. "I'm plum aware of the burden we've allowed ourselves to place on Elijah. But we're at a crossroads now," he said with a long sigh. "I'm a simple man. I don't know where to go from here, and I thought I'd ask you to help me see a way through."

Oren linked his hands behind his back, his mind heavy with thought. "I appreciate that you reached out to me, John. First, let me say that after you left the kitchen that day, I had a long talk with Elijah. He feels not just a sense of responsibility to Jamie, but it's quite clear he is genuinely fond of him. A strong bond has forged between them. It may be a burden, but it's a burden of loyalty and love as well."

"I don't doubt that for a minute. But things are different now. Martha insists that Elijah wants to be in two places, and it's plum clear we're standing in his way."

Oren stopped in the road, turned, and touched John's arm. "Elijah will not leave until Jamie is on his feet, of that I feel certain. But the letting go must come from Jamie. The well-being of your son, which we all want, will only come about when he himself releases the fear and grief that he still holds."

"Reverend, I'm not sure we can force that to happen. He's a mind of his own, my son."

A flock of Canada geese honked overhead, swooped low, and began their gracious descent. Both men paused, grateful for the momentary distraction, and watched as the large birds landed near a line of shade trees along the river.

"Perhaps we can create the circumstance by which this could come about," Oren said tentatively.

"Reckon I ain't following."

"I've been thinking of ways to help you out since my visit. Did you know that the federal government is weighing the idea of distributing confiscated or abandoned land in the South to the emancipated slaves?"

"I may have read something about that."

"Well, the schools we're establishing in the South will prepare freed slaves for work in some of the basic trades and crafts as well as teaching them reading, writing, and arithmetic. Tens of thousands of slaves worked the lands, but had no responsibility for management of the farmlands. Your friend Harry Warren triggered an idea when he said he was learning from you how to efficiently run a farm. My first thought had been to find a way to have the federal government give Elijah a plot of land near the school in Harper's Ferry. If you and your family could live there, even if it were only temporary, you could teach the colored people all aspects of farm management. That way everyone could have been together, Elijah could work something out with his father, and, well, his woman friend—"

"There's a woman involved?

Oren sighed. "Only if she will wait for Elijah, but yes, he cares a great deal for her. Apparently they've known each other since childhood."

John's stride, a reflection of his anxiety, hastened, and Oren walked at a faster pace to stay beside him.

Oren stayed silent for a moment and then said, "Securing a plot of land for Elijah, however, would have been complicated, and now it appears my idea may not work regardless. Senator Fessenden told me that our new president, Johnson, may veto any such legislation."

"Reverend, I appreciate what you were trying to do. But I have my own farm to run. Maine is my home. It's all I know."

Hearing the firmness in John's words, Oren pushed any further talk of exploring the idea aside. Even if in the end, the federal government distributed land, it appeared that John Laird was not about to move his family South.

As they walked, Oren was steeped in thought. Suddenly he stopped. John turned, stopped and looked him squarely in the face.

"Perhaps there is another option. In some ways a better one. I've been working out a plan with my trustees to recruit former slaves to attend school here. My hope is to find some people who have at least a modicum of education, so as to make it a little easier for them, but I'd like Elijah to be one of our students. I'd need to arrange for a student tutor, however, who could work with him and bring him up to speed. Underneath all his shyness, he's a very bright young man."

The train whistled its approach, slowing into the station.

"That's a right kind offer, but it don't solve the dilemma of his wanting to go home."

"No, but perhaps it buys us time while we work this through. Jamie would get used to Elijah being away from home. And we should start slowly, perhaps have Elijah here only two days a week."

"I've no money to spare," John said, his voice a near whisper. Too embarrassed to face the reverend, he watched as people disembarked and hurried along the platform.

"This is my idea, and I'll absorb the costs. Elijah can stay with my wife and me on the nights he is here. But again, it only begins Jamie's separation from Elijah and no more."

"Do you think this could work?"

"With God's help, we can only try."

"You are offering too much, Reverend. And I've no way to repay you."

"Repay me, John? A solution is reward enough."

Oren reached for John's hand. "Ironic, is it not, that here we stand again at another train station? The day I met you, standing on the station platform in Fredericksburg, I became involved."

John saw his hand and took it.

"God put me in your path. His reason is now clearer to me."

"To educate a man is to unfit him to be a slave."
—Frederick Douglass

CHAPTER 30
July, 1865

Elijah stirred in his chair, rubbing his calloused hands over his pants, unable to steady his nerves. Jamie sat calmly beside him, looking at the line of paintings decorating the walnut-paneled walls. Neither spoke.

A flurry of footsteps, a doorknob turning. The door wisped open.

Oren stepped through the threshold, holding back the door and gesturing at Martha and John to take their seats at the long oak table. Behind them walked a young man dressed in a crisp white shirt and dark pants. His light brown hair curled high over his forehead, and his hazel eyes, warm and friendly, darted between Elijah and Jamie.

"Elijah," began Oren, "let me introduce you to Albert Cobb, who will be your tutor." Albert easily walked the distance to greet Elijah, who stood and hurriedly wiped the wetness of his palms against his trouser leg. He met Albert's hand, glanced briefly at him and lowered his gaze.

"And Albert, you must also meet Jamie, the youngest member of the family who has served as Elijah's tutor," he said with a knowing grin at the Lairds.

Pushing back his chair, Jamie stood and shook Albert's hand. "Nice to meet you, Albert," he said, without a hint of nervousness in his voice.

"I'm pleased to meet you both," responded Albert. "And I'm looking forward to working with you, Elijah."

"I think the six of us can begin our discussion of what this tutoring for Elijah will involve," said Oren, motioning everyone to his seats. "Albert is in his second year here. Albert has always been actively involved in the Freewill Baptist Church, and even as a younger man, he spoke fervently against slavery." Oren turned his face to Elijah. "He feels honored to have this unique opportunity to work with you, and to assist you with the education you so deserve."

A blush rose in Albert's cheeks.

"Well, let's have a go at it, shall we?" Oren looked at Albert and said, "Why don't you tell us how this will all come about."

"Certainly, sir. Elijah, it's important for you to know that we will work at a pace that is comfortable for you. It will involve just you and me, for at least four hours each day that you are here. We'll go over a schedule together a little later. In time, there will also be opportunities for you to sit in a classroom as an observer. It will be my responsibility to determine the most appropriate classes for you to attend. But to begin, so that I might prepare for our tutoring lessons, I'll need to know your reading level, your abilities in math and in writing. It will be our starting point."

Elijah stole a glance at Jamie, his eyes wide with bewilderment. How to answer such a question?

"Since I've been doing the teaching, Albert," said Jamie, his voice full with authority, "I can tell you about the learning Elijah's had."

Albert looked questioningly at Oren, who nodded his head in approval.

"He reads some from my school books. I reckon he's reading about like Freddie Marston. He's a really smart fourth grader at my school. And Ma reads the Bible out loud to us most nights. But then she makes Elijah read them same passages back to her."

"So then, and my question is to both of you," Albert added, "how are the words recognized?"

"We sound them out," Jamie answered quickly. "That's important to learning."

"Jamie, suh, he break all them words into little pieces. Then Elijah got to put them all back together and make it so."

"Excellent," said Albert smiling. "Let's move on for now. Tell me about writing." Although he looked to Elijah for a response, Jamie again answered.

"We've been through the alphabet. He knows the letters and can write some. But he still needs my help. His spelling ain't so good yet."

"Elijah spell his name and then some."

"It sounds as if you're motivated to learn. It's hard work, but as I said, we will go slowly and I'll not give you more than you can handle. I would not want to hold back your enthusiasm."

"Oh, Elijah and me take little rests from all the learning," said Jamie. "Sometimes we stop and play a game of checkers and then go back to it."

"I'll remember that," answered Albert. "It's good to know these things. And what about arithmetic?"

"Jamie, suh, he teach Elijah arithmetic with them apples."

"Apples?" asked Albert.

"Yes, suh. First time he try, he go and line all them apples on the fence rail. Then Jamie, suh, he take some apples away and have Elijah learn subtraction."

"Seeing things makes learning easier," added Jamie. "Elijah likes arithmetic. He's right good at it. I'm thinking it comes easier for him."

"Adding, subtracting, and what about multiplying?" Albert fixed his gaze on both.

"Well—" Jamie's face flushed pink and he squirmed in his chair. "Reckon it depends on how many apples we got." He started to giggle; Elijah poked Jamie in the arm.

"Boys!" said John Laird sternly.

Smiling, Oren interrupted and said, "I think our main purpose today was to get acquainted with one another. Albert, you can continue to establish a baseline of Elijah's academic abilities at your next meeting. I suggest we work out a schedule, have some lunch, and then Albert and I will walk you all to the train station."

"It does not matter much whom we live with in this world,
but it matters a great deal whom we dream of."
—Willa Cather, American author

CHAPTER 31

Pappy walked down the row of cabins, the morning sun already warm on his back. He searched the sky, hoping to spot storm clouds gathering in the west to soak the drying fields.

He had grown concerned about Talitha, and before he headed for a long day in the fields, he decided to look for her. She hadn't come by to see him for two days, which was unusual, and he worried she might be ill. When he reached her small, tidy yard, he stopped and stared. A lump formed in his throat. Jackson was holding Talitha's hand, and after a light kiss to her lips, said his good-bye. Smiling, Jackson backed away, nearly bumping into Pappy, and making no apologies, smirked as he strutted by.

Pappy turned around. He had seen enough.

"Pappy Sol, wait! Don't go!" Talitha ran up beside him. "It ain't all what you think."

"Tell me, child, what it is I be thinking?" he said in a firm voice as he kept walking.

"Pappy Sol, you know Jackson been after me a long time. I always push him away, waiting on my Elijah." Talitha crossed her arms, hugging her shoulders, rushing to keep up with his hurried stride. "Then Elijah come back and he leave me. Jackson a good man. I knows you don't like him, but he all right to me."

"You love this boy?"

Talitha took a long breath. "No. Fond of him, is all. Only ever kissed him a few times. And my heart don't catch fire like when I with my Elijah."

"But you gone marry this fool?"

"I don't know. What I knows is that I'm sad and I'm lonely. And Elijah ain't coming back. And Jackson, well, he here."

They walked the rest of the way in silence.

A flock of hens, pecking at the ground, clucked and scattered out of the way as cabins emptied of laborers heading for the fields. Pappy glanced again at the cloudless sky and shook his head. The day would be miserably hot and dusty; no rain in sight.

They reached his cabin. He stopped and turned to Talitha, his eyes filled with sadness.

"You givin' up on my boy?"

"You tell me if he coming back?"

"You know I can't answer that, child."

"Then what do you know?" she shouted angrily.

"I know when love be right." He took both her hands in his. "If I had to wait for my Elisha, however long it take, then nothing ever go and change that. They nobody else make my heart all afire. You only gets that kind of love one time, child."

He sniffed and took a long, deep breath. "And it better than all the years sleeping beside someone who just there."

Talitha fell into his arms. And sobbed. Pappy held her close, blinked back the tears welling in his eyes.

*"Intelligence and courtesy not always are combined;
Often in a wooden house a golden room we find."*
—Henry Wadsworth Longfellow

CHAPTER 32
July, 1865

Oren stood in the back of the classroom observing his friend Reverend Brackett lead his students, all former slaves, in a reading exercise. He listened in turn as each student read a page out loud before handing the book off to the next.

"Halleluiah," shouted an older man as a young woman finished reading a long passage without stumbling, her diction flawless and sharp.

Oren loved the unbridled energy in the room, the friendly cajoling, clapping of hands, all in support of one another, the words of encouragement when one faltered. While the students laughed easily, visibly enjoying the experience, they listened with impassioned respect to their teacher. As an educator, Oren could not help but draw the stark contrast of Brother Brackett's classroom culture to that of his own, where formality and discipline was the standard in New England classrooms. With the exercise completed, and wanting to assess their reading comprehension, the teacher directed the class to pen their thoughts. The students hastily lowered their heads and at last fell silent.

Oren stepped from the room, closing the door quietly behind him. He walked along the wraparound porch of the three-story Lockwood House, mesmerized by the tranquil beauty of Harper's Ferry. Loosening his collar, his shirt damp with sweat from the stifling humid air, Oren nevertheless felt a satisfying peace. Here was the site of the northern abolitionist John Brown and his raid against slavery; here the northern army surrendered the town and its Union garrison after the massive assault from General "Stonewall" Jackson and his army. Now the guns of war were silent. How quickly the earth reclaims itself, thought Oren as he gazed at the lush green river valley. Yet the war-ravaged town lay in ruins, and for its people, the scars would be ageless.

He heard Nathan Brackett call out to him.

"I was delighted to see you come into the classroom. I'd expected you today, and had hoped you would have the chance to see a class in progress." Nathan gave Oren a warm handshake and settled himself on the porch rails. "How were your fundraising efforts in New York and in Washington?"

"My donor visits proved fruitful, and as I often try to do I visited with many prospective students along the way—a part I look most forward to." His eyes brightened as he said, "It did my heart good to see your students' jubilant faces; they are clearly benefiting from the work you are doing."

"God's work. The return is great." Nathan could not help but smile. "When I received your letter asking for possible students to attend Bates this fall, I began a search immediately. I have two men who expressed an interest—Alexander Sanders and Hamilton Keyes, both from Virginia. Bear in mind that most of the freedmen were not open to leaving this area, so that narrowed the candidates considerably, that and trying to find individuals who are better equipped with their academic abilities at this early juncture." Nathan stood and stretched his back. "You'll meet them at supper tonight. Both have interesting stories to tell."

"I'm sure they do."

"I think they are ideal candidates for you, Oren, and they seem quite intrigued about going to Bates."

"I'm looking forward to meeting them."

Nathan smiled slyly. "Oh, and by the way, there will be a number of students gathering later in the evening. I told them we had a guest lecturer that no one should miss hearing."

"Guest?"

"They will love what you have to say."

Early the next morning Oren walked to the train station and purchased a ticket to Salisbury, North Carolina, relieved to learn the rail line was now complete. It was to be his last visit and perhaps his most challenging before he headed back to Maine. The morning air felt cool on his skin, but he knew that within a few short hours the day would turn uncomfortably warm. As he waited on the platform, he thought about the previous night's dinner, the two potential students, and his own message later to the filled room. He had immediately taken to the young men, Alexander Sanders from Fortress Monroe and Hamilton Keyes from Front Royal, candidly answering their questions—where would they live, how would they pay for school, what was it like in Maine, how cold did it get in winter? By evening's end, both had affirmed their desire to travel with Oren to Maine. Oren told them he would be back in two days time and that he hoped to have another student join them as well. His musings kept him occupied and within a short time he heard the whistle, the clatter of wheels as the train pulled into the station. Finding a seat, he sat down, lowered his head, and in minutes was asleep.

The conductor nudged Oren awake. "Your station."

"Thank you, sir." Oren stood slowly, stretched his arms and legs to shake the sleep from his body. Disembarking, he went immediately to the ticket office.

"I'm looking for a large farm owned by a man named Ramsey. Would you know where it is?"

The ticket master looked at him quizzically, as if to inquire about his business at the Ramsey farm, but a line of passengers was quickly forming behind the stranger. "Go straight through town. When you reach a crossroads, take the road to the right. Ramsey farm is beyond, after a long bend in the road."

Oren debated whether to head out, given it was already well into the afternoon, but his anxious nerves pushed him along. He estimated he had walked nearly two miles when he came to the crossroads, and taking a long breath in the oppressive heat, he slowly made his way, veering off to the right, pleased he was almost there.

In the fields, curious workers paused and stared at the stranger walking down Ramsey's lane, a suit coat draped over his arm. When Oren neared the farmhouse, he stopped and asked an older colored man to direct him to Solomon Hall. The man hesitated before he spoke. "Solomon most like in his cabin. He din work the fields today." And pointing his finger said, "All us live in them slave quarters back of the barn. Solomon's cabin the one by the live oak." Rubbing a hand over his chin, he asked, "He done sumthin' wrong, suh?"

"No, not at all. Thank you kindly." As Oren walked past the line of deteriorating one-room wooden cabins, he was struck by the thought that the structures provided little shelter from the cold or the intense heat. Fire pits were just steps away from each door, yet he saw nothing more than an occasional pot or hollowed out gourd for cooking.

Solomon Hall tossed granules of corn at the clucking hens, stopped suddenly when he saw the white stranger coming his way. "Lordy, this about my boy!" A sharp pain ripped through his chest.

"Mr. Hall? Solomon Hall?" Oren said, quickly offering a warm smile to dispel the fear he saw in the man's face.

"My boy, sumthin' happen to my boy?"

"Elijah's fine, Mr. Hall. He's fine." Wiping sweat from his brow with his handkerchief, and spotting stools near the door, Oren asked, "May I sit with you?"

Solomon nodded, working a hand across his chest.

The two sat down in silence.

"Name's Oren Cheney. I'm a minister from Maine. You have a fine son, Mr. Hall. May I call you Solomon?"

Solomon nodded.

"That's why I'm here. To tell you about him."

Oren's smile and easy manner did not relieve the old man's anxiety. "He all right, then?"

"Except for his desire to be here, yes. But let me explain."

Oren talked at length, and as he told him about Jamie, Solomon stopped him and said, "I know about the boy. Elijah don't leave this boy."

"You know then the circumstances of Jamie's grief, and how he looks to Elijah to fill the hole left from his brother's death. He's also very fond of him. And I believe Elijah, who knows from his own childhood the pain of loss, of violence against him, does not want Jamie's scars to define his life. An unselfish act, and I believe he is doing God's work."

Solomon's dark eyes clouded.

"I'm a Freewill Baptist minister, but I'm also president of a college back home. Elijah has a strong desire to learn, and just recently, he has been working with one of my students—"

"My boy in school?" Interrupting, Solomon shook his head in disbelief.

"He's getting help with his primary education from one of my college students. You may be aware that the Freewill Baptists are working with the Freedmen's Bureau to set up schools here in the South to educate your people. I'm down here to recruit former slaves to come to Maine, to my school, if they choose to do that."

"Why you telling Solomon all this? What about my boy?"

Oren laughed out loud. "A fair question. I'm taking far too long to get to my reason for coming here. I know about Talitha, and I was thinking about recruiting her—to come to Maine, to the college."

Solomon looked at him in stunned silence.

"I confess it's all more of a plan to bring Talitha and Elijah together, before it's too late for either of them. In time, they both can return South, to be with you."

Solomon let out a low whistle. "This all complicated now. Mmm-hmm. Talitha, she been all tore up 'bout Elijah leavin' here. She not believing for a minute he come back. Now she taken up with Jackson."

"Oh, my. Is this—" Oren blushed, "am I too late?"

"Hard to say. This the only world she knows. Girl want love and she want a family."

"Do you think she'll speak with me?"

"Talitha ain't gone take kindly to a white folk. Got no reason to."

"I half expected that. But I'd like to try. Would you introduce me to her? I don't want to happen upon Talitha as I did you. I realize I upset you."

Solomon got up from his stool, gazed out across the fields. "Almost sundown. You fixin' on staying, Reverend? Gonna boil a chicken right soon enough. I can borrow a wagon take you back to town for the night."

"I accept your gracious offer."

"Solomon go fetch a chicken."

"Let me do the plucking for you. It's been a long while for me, and I would enjoy the task." Oren stood, folded his suit jacket and placed it on the stool. He rolled up the sleeves of his shirt, smiling to himself.

Solomon built a fire in the earthen pit and set two large water-filled pans on his makeshift stand to boil. He disappeared behind the cabin, returning moments later with a dead chicken. When the water boiled, he plunged the chicken into the pot, pulled it out by its feet and handed it to Oren. Chuckling, he said, "It be easier to pluck them feathers now. This gone be first time I see a white folk clean a chicken. Yes, suh, first time."

Oren laughed with him. "I'll do my best, Solomon."

"We go see Talitha after suppertime."

They worked together in comfortable silence, the initial awkwardness between them fading in the pleasantness of their chores. Smiling his approval, Solomon held the plucked chicken, removed its innards, and placed it in the remaining pan of boiling water. "Them greens is on the kitchen table," he said as he stirred the chicken.Oren nodded and, stepping into the cabin, he could not help but glance at the stark room where Solomon had lived in life. He sighed heavily when he saw the man's bed. Against the back wall, the bed was made out of puncheons fitted on holes bored in the wood. Planks lay across the short poles, and dried corn shucks offered Solomon his only cushion.

Oren scooped the greens up from the table and hurried back outside. He watched as Solomon folded them into the pot, stirred them gently until the sweet smell of collards wafted into their nostrils.

The sun's rays muted into shadows, and beneath the sprawling branches of the live oak the air was slightly more tolerable. Solomon talked easily as he tended to the cooking, and Oren soon found himself enjoying the evening with Elijah's father more than any occasion he could recall in recent memory.

"Tell me about the sharecropping, Solomon. Elijah is concerned for you. How will you be able to handle such a large lot of land largely by yourself?"

Solomon grew quiet, bit down on his lip before he spoke. "Be all right for a time," was all he could muster to say.

"Have you a plow?"

"That boy Harry give me some money. He go and sell them two horses before they takes the train. I try tell him no, suh, Solomon don't take the money but he don't listen. Imagine that. Gone get me a mule and a plow. Yes, suh, the Lord take care of this old man."

"'God is the vine, and ye are the branches,'" said Oren with a faint smile. "'And those that abideth in him, bring much fruit.'"

"Amen, Mr. Cheney. Amen."

"Solomon, this whole idea, I assure you, was to find a way to eventually get Elijah back where he wants to be, with you and, hopefully, with Talitha. He is a very torn young man. Asking Talitha to join him in Maine was the only way I could think of bringing them together. I believe this will open Jamie's eyes, and remove his hold on your son. At least, that's what my thought has been."

"My boy know what you is doing?"

"No, I was too fearful of raising his hopes when I didn't know if the plan would even work." Oren sighed. "And now I have my doubts that it will."

"Mmm-hmm." There was no hint of anger or resentment in Solomon's voice. Perhaps, Oren mused, it was enough for Solomon to know his son was safe and alive.

Solomon stirred the boiling chicken, and seeing the meat fall from the bone, he carefully removed the carcass and set it into an empty gourd.

"Elijah was a boy when they sold him, took him away from me. He a good worker in the fields. Why he wantin' all this learnin' when he just a farmer?"

"Elijah loves working the land. He is at heart a farmer, but he's young, and has seen enough of the white man's world to understand the importance of reading and writing. As a free man, he will need those skills now. A new day has begun, Solomon, a new day."

"Yes, suh, sure enough." Solomon glanced again at the pot. "This chicken all cooked. Plucked by white folk for an old colored. Yes suh, this a new day."

"If a man cannot do everything, he can do something.
If he cannot be faithful in much, he can be faithful in little."
—Oren B. Cheney
Emeline Cheney, *The Story of the Life and Work of Oren B. Cheney*

CHAPTER 33

I nsects erupted in the fields, their nighttime trills like a symphony as Oren and Solomon strolled down the long row of quarters to Talitha's cabin. Although the evening air was warm, small fires burned in the earthen pits, the low flames lighting the darkness as families relaxed together on their meager porches. A lone fiddler offered a smile as he practiced his jig, his wide nostrils flaring, his feet tapping rhythmically each time he pulled his bow across the belly of the fiddle.

Solomon responded to the curious onlookers with a casual greeting or a wave of his hand. As they neared the end of the row, Oren saw three young women sitting around the fire pit engrossed in animated conversation. A burst of laughter filled the air, an infant rocked in its mother's arms, and all the while a lightly-clothed tot crawled on the ground banging at a cluster of earthenware pots with a long wooden spoon. Sensing a presence, one of the women looked up from the fire, and Oren knew at once that the arresting beauty was Talitha. Her smile at seeing Solomon dissolved into fear when she turned her eyes to the white man standing beside him.

"Talitha," said Solomon softly, "this man be a friend of Elijah."

"He here, Pappy Sol? Elijah here?"

"No, child, Elijah still in Maine, where this man from. But you needin' to listen to what he got to say." The other women rushed to their feet, one swooped the toddler in her arms, and without a backward glance, hurriedly walked away, losing themselves in the surrounding darkness.

"His name be Mister Cheney." Solomon turned to leave.

"Pappy Sol! Don't leave me with this white folk."

His voice was soft. "He a man of God, child. Don't you worry now, you hear. He gone help us. But this not for me to listen."

Oren lowered his head and spoke quietly. "May I sit down?"

Talitha stiffened, arched her back, her eyes refusing his. "They ain't no one can help," she finally said. "Sit if you wants."

Seeing her discomfort, Oren picked up a stool and moved it further away from her before he sat down. Fearing she might flee, he chose his words carefully.

"Elijah told me about you, Talitha." Despite the anger resting on her face, her body quivered at his words.

"Elijah make his choice."

"Not entirely, Talitha. He is wretched with conflicting desires, but only because he is trying to do what he believes is right. He very much wants to be with you, and with his father." Oren paused to let his words sink in.

"Why you come?"

"I promised Elijah I would try to help him."

"He know you here?" For the first time, Talitha looked at him, her expression softened by curiosity.

"No, he doesn't know. I came because I have something to offer you, an idea that may help you both."

"I got no reason to trust a white folk. How I know you telling me the truth?"

Oren hesitated, and then with a slight smile said, "Elijah told me when he saw you again that he thought you more beautiful than a spring morning."

"Oh, Lordy," she whimpered. "It him."

"I understand that you have had no reason to trust the white man. And for most of Elijah's life that was also true. But God put in Elijah's path a white man who saved his life. His name was Billy. He was executed by firing squad for deserting the Union army. Elijah is still with us because of him. And now it's this man's younger brother whom Elijah is trying to save."

Talitha sat quietly, and Oren noticed her shoulders slumped from their stiffened pose. "I want to be the white man God puts in your path."

Leaning over, he picked up a stick and poked at the embers in the fire pit. "My parents sheltered runaway slaves in our home, helping them with safe passage to Canada. Sometimes my father would let me lead a runaway on a hidden path through the woods to the next station."

Talitha quickly wiped her tears with the back of her hand. "You done that?"

"Since I was a boy. I knew every inch of those woods, and my father trusted me to guide them safely. Do you know of Frederick Douglass?"

"I know one time he a slave then he escape. He go around and talk about our people."

"Douglass was a friend of my father, and visited us at our home. Through the years, I've remained in touch with him."

"Frederick Douglass your friend?" Talitha was taken back.

He glanced at her and hoped her face might intimate acceptance, bridge a connection. "I feel as if I'm guiding you through the woods, wanting you to trust my judgment that I'll get you where you need to be—with Elijah."

Talitha stood and paced into the darkness, came back and circled the fire pit, arms crossed against her chest. Minutes passed before she sat down.

"What you asking me to do, mister—"

"Cheney."

"Mister Cheney?"

For over an hour Oren told her of the events unfolding in Maine. Talitha bristled when he asked her to return with him, to be a student at his college.

"Solomon told me about Jackson. Perhaps this now affects your decision."

"You don't know nuthin' about Jackson." Talitha fidgeted uncomfortably on her stool. "I ain't even told Pappy Sol yet." Biting down on her tongue, she said, "I told Jackson I ain't marrying him."

Oren tried hard to hide his relief.

She paused, turned and met his eyes. "Elijah need to be here, Mister Cheney. Pappy Sol gonna get hisself a mule and a plow, but he not strong no more. Ramsey say he take the land from Pappy Sol when he start this sharecropping if he don't farm good. Give to another cropper come next season. Then what he do?"

Oren sighed deeply. "We must trust in the Lord, Talitha."

"I don't know, Mister Cheney. I all afeared."

"God is offering you a path through the woods, my child, just as in the Bible, when Gods tells us in Psalm 78 he made his own people go forth like sheep, and guided them in the wilderness like a flock and led them to safety."

He knew he could say no more. He stood. "It's late and you have much to think about. I've not given you any time, for which I am deeply sorry. But I must take the train in the morning to Danville and then on to Harper's Ferry, and there I will be at the Lockwood House for another day. In the event I don't see you tomorrow at the train station, I'll leave money with Pappy Sol for you tonight in hopes that you might change your mind in the days ahead. There are two other students, former slaves, who will be with me. If you decide to join us tomorrow, you wouldn't be traveling alone with me. I know you'd feel more comfortable with companions."

He took a last glance at her.

"I want no less for you than for Elijah."

Talitha only stared at the fire, the dying embers fading to ash.

*"What you need to know about the past is that no matter
what has happened, it has all worked together to bring you to
this very moment. And this is the moment you can choose to
make everything new. Right now."*
—Author Unknown

CHAPTER 34

It was close to midnight when Pappy pulled the wagon to a stop in
front of Salisbury's largest hotel. Bone weary, Oren was relieved to
find a room still available and made a hasty retreat to the four-posted
bed, burying himself in its cool linen coverings.

He awoke to the early sounds of a city preparing for its day, and
outside his door, travelers chatted and scurried down the hotel's narrow
hallway. Looking at his pocket watch, he tossed the bed covers aside and
hurried to dress.

Oren bought a hot buttered biscuit from a bakeshop next to the hotel
and ate it hungrily as he moved along the bustling streets to the station.
He wondered if Talitha would be waiting, or would arrive in Harper's
Ferry within the next day, or would not come at all. Knowing he had
to return to Maine without further delay, he bemoaned the fact that
he had been unable to leave Talitha more time to make so momentous
a decision. The only world she had ever known was contained within
the Ramsey farm, and as much as she professed her love for Elijah, he
prayed she would take this courageous step, Elijah her only thread of
continuity. He allowed himself some consolation in that the seed had at
least been planted, and even though she might not be at the station, there
was always the chance that she might appear unexpectedly in Maine over
the coming weeks. With that hopeful thought in mind, Oren breathed
deeply the fresh morning air, the bank of clouds offering relief from the

increasing humidity.

He turned the last corner before the station. A milk wagon passed in front of him, and when the way was clear, he stepped into the street.

Midway across, Oren saw them.

"Solomon, Talitha," he said, his voice raw with emotion as he hurried to their wagon. "I'm so pleased that you chose to come, Talitha. It is more than I hoped, and I feel almost as anxious as you to see Elijah's face."

Talitha tried to smile. She wore no head wrap, and her hair coiled into a loose bun; coppery ringlets fell from her brow. Her calico dress was patterned with small blue and white squares, and a line of white lace framed its high neckline.

Clutching Solomon's hand, she said, "Where them other coloreds, Mister Cheney? You say they gone travel with us."

"Alexander Sanders and Hamilton Keyes will meet up with us at Harper's Ferry. We'll be together for the longer journey."

Talitha nodded. "I ain't never been further than Salisbury or Durham, Mister Cheney. I need my own folk."

"I understand. We have only a few hours on this coach. It's important to me that you are comfortable."

Solomon sighed. "And it don't help none that that fool Jackson show up this morning making all them promises to her."

"Pappy Sol—"

"Oh, I hush up now." He glanced at the sky, pleased to see it growing darker. "Storm clouds gathering. Corn's finally gone get their water come afternoon."

"To every thing there is a season, Solomon," Oren said, still smiling as he reached into the tailboard and pulled out Talitha's bulky cloth bag.

Solomon stepped down from the wagon, walked to the opposite side, and reached for Talitha's hand as she eased herself to the ground. His eyes misted. She was the daughter he never had the chance to know. Lydia was barely a day old when she died, smothered in her mother's arms so "that she don't grow up a slave," an all-too-common practice during the harsh years of slavery. Although his heart had been broken, Solomon had understood the painful decision his wife had made.

"Mister Cheney, you watch out for my chilluns," he said, rubbing his eyes with the back of his hand.

"Of that you can be sure, my friend."

"That all Solomon ask."

The station was unusually quiet; few travelers mingled on the platform. Oren purchased another ticket, refusing Solomon's attempt to return the money he had given him earlier for Talitha's fare. "Keep it and buy yourself a good mattress today while you have the wagon. It's time your tired bones not lay on dried corn shucks across a plank board."

Solomon shook his head. "That what Mastuh Fowler tell me. Ain't never slept on no mattress afore."

"Pappy Sol—" Talitha cried out, her lips quivering as she gazed down the length of the station platform. Solomon followed her frightened stare.

Jackson stood a short distance away, hands resting on his hips. Then his eyes met hers.

Sensing something was suddenly terribly wrong, Oren turned to Solomon.

"Jackson be here, Mister Cheney. Talitha got all this fear going and now he go and play on it." Oren spotted the striking, broad-shouldered man, his eyes firmly fixed on Talitha. In spite of his strong posture, his face conveyed sadness, his dark eyes pleading.

"Pappy Sol—"

"Child, he not making this easy for you. Just close your eyes and ask if this be the man you want."

"Listen to your heart, Talitha, not your fear," added Oren in a most gentle tone.

Talitha pinched her eyes closed, took several deep breaths and tried to calm her anxious nerves. Seconds passed. She hastened another look at Jackson and then quickly averted her eyes.

"Put me on this train, Pappy Sol. I knows what I want."

"That my girl." From the corner of his eye, Solomon saw Jackson closing the gap between them. Placing a hand on Talitha's shoulder, he turned her quickly toward the rail car.

"Solomon! No! Don't let her go!"

"Step yourself back, Jackson," Solomon said. "She gone be with my boy."

"You sending her off with a white folk?" he shouted, glaring at Oren. "Only harm go and come to her, you ol' fool."

"Jackson, please, I know that you—" Oren stammered.

"This between my people."

"Let's go, Talitha," Jackson ordered. He turned and grabbed her hand before she had a chance to resist. Talitha moaned, twisted her body.

Solomon flung his thin body, arms outstretched, at Jackson, but he was no match against the virile young man, who with one arm easily pushed the old man in his chest. Solomon stumbled, fell backward, and landed hard on the platform, the back of his head cracking against the wood.

"Pappy Sol! Pappy Sol!" Talitha wretched her hand free and with Oren, dropped down beside Solomon.

"May God forgive you your unmerciful actions, Jackson," said Oren as he carefully raised Solomon's head and examined the back of his skull.

"I here, Pappy Sol," Talitha cried.

"I all right. This ol' head's too hard no how."

"There's no open wound, my friend," said Oren, "but you've a nasty bump nevertheless."

Talitha glared at Jackson. "Get yourself gone. I ain't never go and be with you. Never!"

Jackson backed away, his face still raw with anger. "This all your fault, Solomon. You pay someday, you pay." As the train whistled its imminent departure, Jackson turned and walked into the crowd of curious spectators who quickly moved out of his way.

Oren let out a large sigh and with Talitha, eased Solomon onto his feet.

"Are you sure you're all right, Solomon?"

"Solomon all fine," he answered, wiping the dust from his pants. "Jackson, he nuthin' but talk. Be chasing 'nuther skirt soon enough."

"Most like that be Sadie," said Talitha, trying to lighten his spirits, if not her own. Tenderly she brushed the dirt from the back of Solomon's shirt. "Ain't gone be around now to do your washing." She took a deep breath. "This all so hard, Pappy Sol—leaving you. And what if Elijah all mad I come?"

Pappy Sol leaned over and kissed her on her forehead. "This what Solomon want for you. And you and Elijah gone be fine. You just need to get there, child. Then this all work out."

"All aboard!"

Talitha reached for her bag, not willing to take another look down the platform.

"I loves you, Pappy Sol."

"I loves you, too, little one. You tell my boy Pappy give his blessing. Tell him this all good."

Oren reached for Solomon's hand. "Peace be with you."

"And you, suh. Maybe I go and get that mattress afore the rain come. Like you say, Mister Cheney, this a new day. And it belong to my chilluns."

"The pain of parting is nothing to the joy of meeting again"
—Charles Dickens

CHAPTER 35
August, 1865

Elijah headed down Cranberry Meadow Road, his schoolbooks under his arm. The morning air was warm; thin clouds pockmarked the pale blue sky. A lone cow looked up from its grazing as he walked by, swished her tail at flies, and meandered away from the fence.

"Elijah, wait!"

Elijah stopped, turned and waited as Jamie ran up to him. "Where you going this all-fired early, Jamie, suh?"

"Nowheres," he answered coyly, catching his breath. "I mean, I went and told Ma I was walking to the train with you."

"But you ain't?"

"Maybe some, I mean, at least part of the way." Jamie kicked a clog of dirt, scattering dust in the air, and sneezed when it settled in his hair.

"Mmm-hmm. You tell Elijah what this 'maybe' all about."

Biting down on his lower lip, Jamie took a long, slow breath. "I'll tell you, but you needin' to promise not to tell Ma." He took a deep breath. "Got me a new friend."

"What kind of friend?"

"Just a girl, is all."

"What her name?"

"Emma. Been talking to her after Sunday school." He tugged on Elijah's shirt. "You won't tell?"

"No, suh." He put a reassuring hand on Jamie's shoulder. "But you needin' to let Elijah know."

"I'm meeting up with her at Blaisdell's Store. Her ma works there when Harriet can't come. Emma said she would give me some licorice strings." Jamie kicked at a stone this time and watched it fly into the air.

Elijah laughed. "What you liking more, this Emma or them licorice strings?"

"Hard to say." Jamie scrunched his nose. "You ever kissed a girl?"

"You still a chillun. Don't be talking foolish now."

"Just asking, is all."

Elijah stared into the distance, the question pulling images from the back recesses of his mind. A hawk circled overhead, then swooped low over the fields.

"Billy, suh, he ask me same thing one time."

"He did?"

"Yes, suh. Elijah tell him he go and kiss a girl in a cornfield."

Jamie giggled. "What was her name?"

"Talitha," he said, her name catching in his throat.

"You only kissed her one time?"

"Never mind this talk, or Elijah follow you and meet Miss Emma."

"Anyways, that's a pretty name, Talitha."

Elijah took a deep breath, stared aimlessly at the cows grazing in the pasture, half-wishing he was back in the barn, milking the herd.

"You thinking you'll still be a farmer after all this learning?"

"It all Elijah know, Jamie, suh. Someday maybe Elijah go and be a preacher, like Mistah Cheney."

"He wanted to take you away from me." Jamie reached for Elijah's hand, kicked again at the pebbled road.

"Jamie, suh, we been through this. Mistah Cheney, he thinking he do right."

Jamie shrugged his shoulders. "Elijah?"

"What, child?"

"If you move South, can I come live with you?"

"Elijah ain't movin' South."

"But if you do?"

"Then what about Miss Emma?"

"Oh, I forgot."

Their shared laughter lifted in the wind.

Elijah stepped off the train in Lewiston. His lessons with Albert had been going well, and most of the time he looked forward to his tutoring in spite of the frustration he felt when he did not easily grasp all that was being put before him.

Two students stood on the platform and as he passed by, one of them called out to him. "Good morning. We've seen you around campus. If you're going that way now, mind if we walk with you?"

"That be fine," Elijah answered, surprised at how easily the words rolled off his tongue.

"We heard that President Cheney's been recruiting former slaves to attend Bates. But you've been coming here for a while now. Were you always a free man?"

Elijah shook his head. "No, suh. Elijah escape from Danville, Virginia. Then go to Canada."

"I'd like to hear about that sometime, if that's all right with you."

"All right, suh."

"So you're Elijah. My name's Peter, and this is my friend Isaac."

They exchanged smiles.

"President Cheney's supposed to be back later today. Fidelia says he was hoping to be bringing maybe two or three freedmen with him," said Isaac.

"I think they'll be coming from that school in Harper's Ferry," added Peter.

His words hit Elijah hard. He felt the pull across his chest and forced himself to bury the emotions welling within. The school. Talitha. Pappy.

When they reached Hathorn Hall, Elijah made his good-bye, walked into the conference room and waited for Albert. His mind not yet quieted, he opened his book, hoping to lose himself in its words.

"I'm impressed with your reading, Elijah. You did extremely well today." Albert reached for his satchel and pulled out another book. "I'd like you to work on the first chapter of this next book, *Moby Dick*. It's not the easiest read, but I think you'll find the story interesting."

Albert stood, gathered the last of his papers, pushed them into the satchel and prepared to leave. Then he hesitated, and sat back down.

"Elijah, this is not easy to bring forth, but perhaps it's time."

"What that be?"

"As we begin your writing lessons, you need to understand that writing often reflects one's manner of speaking. I think it's time we work together to correct your speech, if that's all right with you?"

"What be wrong with how Elijah speak, Albert, suh?"

"The most important improvement or change you need make is in how you refer to yourself. It should be in the first person."

"What you mean first person?"

Albert paused, cleared his throat. "When we refer to ourselves, we use the first person, such as the word 'I.' We don't use our name. For example, you would begin a sentence by saying 'I like to read' rather than saying 'Elijah like to read.'"

Elijah lowered his gaze. For as long as he remembered, it had always been that way with him. Albert's words struck hard. More than anger, he felt embarrassed, and could not bring himself to look up or respond.

"I'll see you tomorrow then."

Elijah listened to Albert leave the room, the door close behind him. He slumped back in his chair and took a deep breath. Tossed his pencil onto the table. He hadn't really been aware of his speech, or that it was somehow wrong. He thought about the new coloreds arriving on campus. Wondered if they talked as he did. He buried his face in his hands.

Then he heard the door crack open, and hurriedly pushed himself upright in his chair.

"Good. You're still here. And alone," said Oren. Without waiting for Elijah's response, he stepped back from the door as if to let someone pass.

Slowly, Talitha moved across the threshold.

Shock sat on Elijah's face. "Talitha?"

He fumbled with his chair, stood and stared before he ran to her. He was afraid he would crush her, his arms wrapped so tightly around her.

Oren turned to leave.

"Mistah Cheney?" Elijah looked up at him.

"Talitha will tell you all. I'll be in my office," he said starting to leave.

"Mistah Cheney?"

Oren stopped.

"Elijah want to say—" His voice raspy, "say thank you."

"God works in mysterious ways." Oren smiled and this time disappeared into the hall, closing the door behind him.

"Oh, Talitha, how this be?"

"Please tell me you is happy to see me," she said through her tears, resting her head beneath his chin.

"This first time Elijah feel happiness."

"And Pappy Sol, he give his blessing. He say this gone be all good."

"Then we make it so."

He held her and held her until the beating of her heart slowed against his own. Even then he was reluctant to let her go.

Letter from John W. Dungy to William Still, January, 1861.
*"I often think of you all. I pray that the time may come
when we will all be men in the United States. We have read
here of the great disturbance in the South. My prayer is that
this may be a deathblow to slavery. Do you ever have any
Underground Railroad passengers now? Times have been
very prosperous in Canada this year."*
—William Still, *The Underground Railroad*

CHAPTER 36

Talitha emerged from the stately brick house and raced into Elijah's arms.

"I have me a beautiful room! House lady say I be sharing with another girl when she come along. But it all big and so fancy, there plenty of room. Even got curtains on the windows. Long and fine ones like I seen when Mama and me was in the mastuh's house." Tilting back her head, she searched Elijah's face. "Maybe you and me have a room like this one day."

"Elijah promise," he said, his mind still reeling from the shock of seeing her. He pulled her close, letting her warmth envelope him.

"How long you stay afore you goes to the farm?"

"Elijah go tomorrow."

Talitha's body suddenly stiffened, and she broke away from his arms, her hands clasped her cheeks. "Oh, Elijah that ain't near enough time with me! How long you be gone?"

Elijah reached for her trembling hands, cupped them in his. "You want to come with me?"

"They knows about me at all? The boy?"

He shook his head no. "Elijah tell Missus Martha right off. Then

Elijah come back for you."

"How all this go and work? Me having to go to school. Everything all so new. Then you gone most times." She let out a long, lingering sigh. "I have me a beautiful room, but I gots all these fears running through me."

Elijah stopped and pulled her to him. "See how it go, Talitha. See how it go."

"Elijah, I wants to be with you."

"We figure this out soon enough. Elijah never let you go again." For the moment Talitha seemed appeased, as if accepting his words.

"I knows. It all so new for both of us. And I here with you now."

They strolled down to the river and sat on its wide bank away from the bustle and noise of the mills. Elijah handed her his book, *Moby Dick,* and read out loud to her the first page. When he finished, Talitha lifted the book from his hands, leafed through the pages, all the while shaking her head in awe at his ability to read its seemingly endless words.

"Elijah need to ask you something. About this learning. Albert, suh, he tell Elijah to say 'I'. He say it be the first person. Way folks is supposed to talk."

Talitha let forth a small laugh. "Long as I knows you, you don't never say 'I'. Pappy Sol say 'I' from time to time. Some slaves talk as you, some don't. When I growed up in the mastuh's house, they make you talk right." Talitha grinned. "First person."

"Elijah like how he talk."

Talitha laughed. He laughed with her.

"Mister Cheney said we was to come by his office later," Talitha said. "Then I wants you to meet my friends—they our people—Alexander Sanders and Hamilton Keyes. Come with me on the train."

"Elijah, Talitha," called Oren Cheney from his office. "Come in. I'd like you to meet another student who has just arrived."

Fidelia sat at her desk, barely able to contain her joy at seeing Elijah with Talitha. They greeted her warmly and passed into Mr. Cheney's office.

A handsome colored man wearing a neatly trimmed goatee, his skin color light as Talitha's, stood in the middle of the room.

Oren clasped his hands around Elijah's. "Elijah this gentleman, John Dungy, has a story similar to your own. And John, this is Elijah Hall and

Talitha Simms."

John smiled heartily at both. "Mr. Cheney tells me you lived in Canada for a while following your escape—as I did. And I just learned we have something else in common."

"What that be?"

"To begin with, I was hired out by my master to the plantation of John Gregory, Virginia's former governor. But shortly after arriving I learned that he and his family were soon moving to Alabama. I had desired to escape for several years, and realized if I were living further south, an escape would be more challenging. I knew it was my moment to flee. I ran, and fortunately was able to hide on a ship bound for Philadelphia. There I met our mutual acquaintance, William Still."

"Mistah Still?" Memories flashed through Elijah's mind. Still, the free colored man who had searched the streets of Philadelphia looking for him and Billy. Still was the recording secretary for the city's Vigilance Committee, a group of white abolitionists and freemen who interviewed runaway slaves before secreting them on the Underground Railroad to Canada.

"Did you talk with his committee?" John asked.

His question brought him back to the moment. "Yes, suh. Elijah sit at the table long time. They ask me all them questions."

"As they did with me. And Mr. Still penned our answers. Perhaps for history's sake."

"What they ask?" Talitha looked curiously at Elijah and John.

"Mostly about our family, who our owners were. All for the record. And of course, a great deal about our experience as a slave," answered John.

"There one question Mistah Still say committee ask all slaves," added Elijah.

Oren leaned forward. "Interesting. What question was that?"

"They tell Elijah that suppose your mastuh find you after you escape and he say you can choose death on the spot or return to slavery. Then they ask Elijah what he choose."

Oren bit down on his lip. "And your answer?"

"Elijah tell them he cross the waters afore he go back." Talitha hugged her body close to him. He reached for her hand.

Oren turned to John. "And this was asked of you as well?"

"Yes. And my answer was the same."

Oren sighed, turned his face to the window, and held his gaze on the distant thunderheads looming over the Androscoggin River.

"You gone see Mistah Still again?"

John shrugged his shoulders. "Hard to say. We correspond. While I was in Canada, I wrote to him frequently. I was lonely much of the time, and I used that opportunity to write as much as possible."

"Elijah only learning to write. When you write to Mistah Still, you tell him Elijah be here."

"I will indeed. And I look forward to seeing more of you and Talitha."

"Elijah like that."

"Children are the hands of which we take hold of heaven."
—Henry Ward Beecher, abolitionist and clergyman

CHAPTER 37

"**M**istah Cheney?" Elijah poked his head inside the door, pleased to see the reverend was at his desk. Fidelia had not been in the outer office. "Elijah just wantin' to say thank you again for what you done."

Oren beamed as he leaned back in his chair. "I was at my desk writing to Reverend Brackett in Harper's Ferry one afternoon to tell him I would be coming down to look for students. Then I thought of Talitha. It was as if God spoke to me. And I knew at that moment I had to go to Salisbury and see Talitha, to ask her to come here as a student. It was a way for her to be with you."

"Elijah never forget this kindness."

"Remember that day in the Lairds' kitchen? I told you the story of the prophet, and how he saved the boy? You asked if that was how the story ended, and I told you for the prophet, yes. I wanted to find a way to make things work for you, so that your story would not end with just the boy."

"Yes, suh, you make Elijah get to the other side and see happy."

Oren smiled at his words.

"And I also had the pleasure of spending a remarkable evening with your father. Did you know he had me plucking a chicken?"

Elijah smiled. "Yes, suh. Talitha go and tell me."

"I would not have succeeded in bringing Talitha back with me had it not been for his help. An extraordinary man, your father. By the way, have the Lairds met Talitha yet?"

"She come with Elijah today."

"Splendid. And Jamie—does he know about her?"

"Missus Martha, she say wait 'til Talitha come. We tell him then."

"Hmmm."

Elijah's smile faded. He shifted his weight on his feet as Oren studied him.

"I sense there is something bothering you. Are you worried about Jamie?"

Elijah shook his head. "Only some."

"Then what am I hearing now in your voice? Is it school?"

Elijah lowered his gaze.

"Elijah, please. I'm here to listen. It's what I do."

"Why Elijah need to talk different?"

"What do you mean?"

"Elijah got to talk first person. Why that so?"

Oren took a deep breath. "I suspect this is coming from Albert. Elijah, he may be right in what he is trying to tell you. But this is not something you must change immediately if it's uncomfortable for you."

"Why this have to change no how?"

"Education has a unique purpose, Elijah. It broadens our world and helps us to better understand and adapt to the society we live in. You are now a free man, and soon, as an educated man, society will expect you to shed some old ways of the past, as a way of adapting, fitting in. But for now, if you want to refer to yourself not as I, but as Elijah, then so be it."

Elijah nodded, met his eyes.

"Only you will know when that time comes." Oren watched him as he turned to leave.

"It will never take away from who you are, Elijah."

Elijah held Talitha's hand tightly in his as they walked up Cranberry Meadow Road. Although surprised to learn about Talitha, Missus Martha had offered him a ready smile, and had at once insisted he bring her to the farm. He had sensed in her a great empathy for Talitha, who was facing everything new and unfamiliar, and she cautioned Elijah that Talitha would need time to adjust to her surroundings. She felt certain that Talitha would need to be close to him as much as possible, and for that reason, Missus Martha encouraged him to bring Talitha to the farm in hopes she might find it a place of comfort. He had been pleased with her reaction, especially since he wondered still about her, the sadness she held deep inside.

Although anxious, Talitha desired to meet the white family that had treated Elijah as a son. Since her arrival at Bates, Elijah had seen in her a remarkable spirit, her easy way around the other coloreds. Yet in spite of friendly overtures from white students, she remained shy and hesitant with them. Albert had suggested she begin her tutoring slowly, and in the end, she asked only to sit with Elijah during his lessons, to listen and to observe. She had surprised both men at her first meeting when she twice injected an opinion and then sat back in her chair as if waiting to be challenged. For most of their lives together, Elijah had known Talitha as a compliant slave, and this occasional hint of a strong will only deepened his love for her. He likened her to the closed petals on a flower, opening at last, revealing an intrinsic beauty.

"That be the farmhouse, Talitha. Top of the hill."

Elijah felt her small hand squeeze hard in his. "They ain't no reason to be afeard."

"Except maybe the boy," she said hesitantly.

"Remember he only that, a boy."

The scent of roses filled the air along the worn path to the farmhouse porch. Sweet William and monkshead bloomed in splashes of color against the weathered clapboards, and cinnamon rose hugged the ends. Kneeling in her flower garden, pulling at weeds, Martha turned her head at the sound of voices. Raising herself off the ground, she wiped her fingers against her apron and held out her hand. "I'm so happy to meet you Talitha," she said. "I'm Martha."

With a deep breath, Talitha saw Martha's hand and took it. "Thank you kindly, ma'am."

"Let's go inside." Picking her cut flowers off the ground, Martha said, "John's in the barn if you want to fetch him, Elijah."

Talitha glanced nervously as Elijah headed across the barnyard, but Martha placed a hand under Talitha's elbow and gently led her up the stairs. "I've been looking forward to your visit. It will be nice to have another woman to talk with."

Laughter greeted John and Elijah as they entered the house. Curdles of smoke darkened and fouled the air.

"What's burning?" John shouted, hurrying his stride to the kitchen.

In the folds of a thick cloth, Martha held out a pie, its crusted top blackened with ash. "I wanted to show our guest what a fine baker I am," she said. Talitha held her hand over her mouth, and again the women erupted in laughter.

Elijah was quietly pleased that a burned pie seemingly brought them together. He looked lovingly at Talitha, quickly discovering how each situation revealed a new facet of her. He started for the kitchen; it was time to discuss Jamie before he arrived home. Then he heard footsteps running across the porch.

The door pushed open.

"Jamie, suh," Elijah said, greeting him and placing his arm around his shoulder. Warily, Talitha stepped into the sitting room, tried to raise a smile she did not feel.

"Who's she?" Jamie said as he pushed his back into Elijah's chest.

"She my friend."

"Hello," he said shyly, studying her.

"Hello, back, Jamie." A hint of a smile tugged at the edges of Talitha's mouth.

"You a new friend?"

"Well, not so new."

A worried look passed over Jamie's face. "How long you known Elijah?"

"Since I was your age, I'm guessing."

Jamie craned his neck; his eyes shifted from side to side, first at Elijah and then back to the woman.

"What's your name?" he asked, fear rising in his voice.

"I'm Talitha."

"Talitha?" His blue eyes flashed, and he turned a reddening face to Elijah. "The girl in the cornfield!"

"This be her, Jamie, suh."

"Then, she's coming to take you away!" Breaking away from Elijah, he ran from the house, the door slamming behind him.

Elijah started after him.

"No, Elijah, leaves this to me," Talitha said.

"Talitha's right," said Martha quickly. "Let her go instead."

Elijah shook his head. "No, this for me to do."

Martha pulled on the sleeve of his shirt. "Trust her instincts, Elijah.

I do."

"Thank you, ma'am," Talitha said softly as she patted Elijah on the arm. Summoning her will, she headed for the door.

Outside the air was cool, and Talitha shivered more from the unaccustomed chill than her own nerves. One small boy was not going to threaten her chance for happiness.

She found him sitting on the bottom steps, elbows on his knees, his chin cupped in his hands. She sat down beside him. To her relief, he did not move.

"I know about you," he sniffed, wiping his nose against the sleeve of his shirt.

"What you know?"

"He kissed you one time. In the cornfield."

Talitha held back a smile. "He done told you that?"

"Yeah. Elijah tells me everything. He's my brother."

"I knows."

Jamie narrowed his eyes, but he would not look at her. "Did you come to take him away?"

"I came here to be with him, no matter where he go and live." Talitha palmed the wrinkles of her cotton dress.

"Can I tell you something?" she asked in a gentle tone.

"Guess so."

"When Elijah come South to find his pappy, it be the first time I seen him in near three years. I know he run away from Mastuh Fowler. But after he run, Pappy Sol and me thought he dead. But then I go to see Pappy Sol one night and there Elijah be. I thought my heart stop beating I was so happy Elijah alive and that he come home."

"My brother saved him."

"And I praise the Lord he did, every day, Jamie."

"My brother's dead." Jamie sniffed, tears running down his cheeks.

"I knows, and I'm so very sorry because I knows he fought for our freedom."

Talitha looked out across the barnyard, breathed in the flower-scented air, using the moment to collect her thoughts. Jamie lowered his tear-stained face in his hands. Neither spoke; neither moved.

"I been in love with Elijah since I was your age," she said at last.

"He told me I'm too young for all that stuff. But he went and kissed you no how."

Talitha held back her smile. "Maybe for Elijah it only a simple kiss. But it was enough for me to knows what I want. And I waited for him. When he come home, I start to thinking maybe we gone marry. But then he go away. Fast as he came."

Talitha turned to Jamie and said, "Look at me, child."

His lips puckered. She waited for his glance, but none came. "Look at me, I said."

Reluctantly he raised his face. His eyes met hers.

"Elijah go and leave me cause he say he got to be with some boy back in Maine."

"He promised me."

"It more than a promise, Jamie. He make his choice. He say he love me, but he going back. He love you too, promise or no." Talitha's eyes welled, but she refused to cry.

"You knows what I'm saying? Elijah go and choose you over me."

Jamie's face flushed with surprise; he studied her.

"You think that easy to say? Why you think I here? I worry I never see him again." Talitha reached for her square of cotton and blew her nose. "I figure I come here and see if he want me with him. He do, Jamie, but he ain't leaving you just the same."

When Jamie didn't respond, she sat in silence for several moments.

"I want to ask you sumthin', child." Talitha spoke in a near whisper.

"All right."

"You think you can share Elijah with me?"

Jamie bit down on his lower lip. "How you figure?"

"A heart got more'n enough room no matter how much love it get. Elijah never gone love you less just cause you be sharing him with me."

Talitha waited for several moments, hoping for a response as Jamie sat quietly, resting his elbows on his knees. Then he buried his face once again in his hands.

Talitha pushed herself to her feet, hesitated, and walked back into the house.

Elijah tried to read the masked expression on Talitha's face as she headed for the kitchen. Glancing at the front door, he moved to open it.

"Leave him be, Elijah," Talitha said firmly without turning around.

"I started another pie." Forcing a smile she did not feel, Martha followed Talitha into the kitchen. "I've made the dough if you wouldn't mind rolling it out."

"I did my best with him, ma'am."

Martha's face paled; her hands shook. "I'll get the jar of berries."

"Are you all right, ma'am? You all a trembling."

"I'll be fine."

Pulling the dough from the bowl, Talitha shaped it loosely into a ball and set it down on a lightly floured board. Using a small amount of flour she dusted the rolling pin and deftly rolled out the crust.

Footsteps.

"Talitha?" Jamie stood at the edge of the kitchen. His pale blue eyes, although rimmed red, were dry.

Talitha set down the rolling pin and carefully wiped the flour from her hands before she turned to look at him. "Yes, child?"

"I reckon I can share him with you."

"And you ain't gone change your mind?" she said, trying to keep her voice soft, but firm.

"No."

Talitha nodded. "Thank you, Jamie. This all work out, you'll see." She wanted to reach out to him, but instinct cautioned her. Too soon, she told herself. Do not give the child an opening, a chance to retreat from his words.

Talitha hurried a glance at Martha, startled at the sudden change in her softened expression. Her cheeks glowed and a wide smile crossed her face.

Then Martha rushed across the floor and wrapped her arms around her son. "I'm so proud of you." She stroked his wispy brown hair and kissed him on his forehead. "Do you know how much this helps me, knowing what a big step you have taken?"

Jamie nodded and said, "But I have to tell Elijah something."

"Elijah here, Jamie, suh," he said, entering the kitchen.

"It's private."

Elijah placed an arm around his shoulder. "We go over here," he said, leading Jamie into the sitting room where John sat on the sofa, his hands clasped tightly together.

"This is private, Pa."

"Well, then, I guess I'll learn how to make a pie," he answered. With a wink at Elijah, John retreated to the kitchen.

"What you got to tell me?"

"I told Talitha I would share you."

Elijah sighed deeply. "Elijah always here for you, Jamie, suh."

"I know. Talitha said you ain't going to love me less. But there's something else."

"What that be?"

"Thing is, I went and kissed Emma even though you told me not to."

"Mmm-hmm."

"I guess I thought it'd be all right. But then Talitha said she was the same age as me when you went and kissed her."

"Why that so bad, Jamie, suh?"

"Talitha said after you went and kissed her she knew right then she wanted to marry you." Jamie rubbed his hands up and down his trousers. "What if Emma is wanting to go and marry me?" Jamie hung his head. "I should've listened."

Feigning a frown and a sigh, Elijah said, "This a problem Jamie, suh."

"Yeah."

"You sure you don't want this marrying?"

"I'd rather have me the licorice strings."

"It is easier to build strong children than to repair broken men."
—Frederick Douglass

CHAPTER 38
Late August, 1865

Pappy woke from a dream in which he had been drifting on a cloud, feathery and soft, like a sack full of picked cotton. When he opened his eyes, he thought himself still floating. His hand reached down by his side; his long bony fingers, swollen with arthritis, felt the mattress beneath him. "Lord, this be my cloud. Ain't never feel nuthin' like this afore." He wished he had followed Mister Cheney's advice nearly a month ago when he told him to purchase a mattress for his tired bones. But much as he had liked the idea, he hadn't been able to allow himself such unaccustomed luxury. Then yesterday, after limping home from the fields, he borrowed Ramsey's wagon, went to Salisbury, and bought his mattress.

Day was breaking, but he lay still, willing himself a few more precious moments in the comfort of his new bed. There was a time his old master would have told him to get off his cloud and get out to the fields. Now he was a free man, and since Ramsey hadn't yet divided up the land for sharecropping, his only task was to weed his rows of corn. He doubted he would be missed for a while. He smiled when he thought about the corn. Already the stalks were high, promising to be a good crop this year. The rains fell more often now.

He didn't know how long he dozed, and when he wakened again, he knew he must hurry. He hoped no one would notice his lateness. Reluctantly he raised himself from his bed and dressed in a loose shirt and overalls. He moved to the door, stopped and turned around, and took a long, lingering look at his mattress. With a shake of his head, he headed out to the cornfields.

The day was miserably hot and humid, but he never minded the heat baking on his back. He spotted Jackson trailing Sadie, a pretty young woman who seemed more than pleased with his attention. Jackson caught his glance and turned his back. He offered a wry smile that Jackson did not see.

With Talitha gone these many weeks, he reckoned that things must be going well for her up North. How he missed her sweet company. But he took great comfort in knowing she was with his son. In his mind's eye, he imagined his chilluns together, happy, planning a life of endless possibilities now that they were free.

Picking up his hoe, he moved down the old, familiar rows, digging away at the weeds, careful not to nick the young stalks. Suddenly he felt a curious tightening across his chest, then an old, familiar sharp pain. He leaned on his hoe, waited until it passed and then continued on, well into the afternoon.

He was unusually tired, and had missed his noon meal. Perhaps he would stop working soon. As he swatted at an annoying fly, the tightening pulled again across his chest, the pain sharper and more intense. His heart beat rapidly. Instinctively he wanted to massage the pain, but his right hand fell abruptly to his side, numb to his touch. A wave of dizziness overwhelmed him, and nearly stumbling, he eased himself to the ground. He lay still, feeling the moist earth beneath him, the heat pressing down.

When he opened his eyes, he wondered at first where he lay and snapped his head from side to side. Found himself cradled in his cornstalks. He looked up at the sky, the clouds the color of heather, lavender and gray in the waning light.

Almost sundown.

Pain ratcheted his body and he gasped for air. He thought he heard rustling among the stalks, cushioned steps across the yielding earth. Was someone coming? Was help near? How desperately he wanted to be in his cabin again, to feel the cloud-like softness of his mattress beneath him.

The pain intensified, if that was even possible. A long, agonizing groan erupted from his throat. Above him a shadow stood against the dying light. Wincing, he studied the near silhouetted figure.

Jackson.

Using what little strength remained, Pappy raised his head and tried to speak, but his voice failed him. He prayed Jackson would carry him back to his cabin, lay him down on his mattress. But Jackson just stood there, motionless, a silent stare, his large hands buried in the depths of his pockets.

Then, without warning, without uttering a word, Jackson turned and walked away, purposely stomping on the green stalks where Pappy lay.

A single tear trickled down Pappy's cheek. He lowered his head to the ground.

Darkness settled in around him.

The end of a day. *His day?*

He could no longer move any part of his body. His breathing slowed, he felt his spirit lifting from his earthly presence. His last thoughts, fainting like the light, turned to his wife, Elisha. The spread of blue violets decorating her grave, the many years she had been gone from him. Did she know what a fine son they had? He felt blessed that Elijah had come home, that he had survived his tortuous boyhood. He had hoped to see him again. But it was not to be. He reasoned this unexpected twist of fate with grace, content that his son was happy, happier now with Talitha beside him.

Strangely, he felt at peace. He turned again to gaze at the young corn and unable to raise a finger, his mind caressed the trampled stalks.

He closed his eyes.

And drifted peacefully on a cloud.

"Death is the story of Life"
—African proverb

CHAPTER 39

O ren pulled out his chair, sat down, and stared at the stack of papers
on his desk. He had kept his afternoon free of commitment,
needing time in his office to sort through endless paperwork
and to catch up on his mail. He did a quick pass at the pile, separating
internal documents from correspondence, and had nearly completed his
sorting when he spotted a small envelope resting under a large folder.
Picking it up, he turned the envelope over and stared at the return
address: Salisbury, North Carolina. He felt a twinge in his stomach, and
with a sense of foreboding, he reached for his letter opener, carefully
slit open the envelope along its seam, and pulled out a single sheet of
stationery and several dollar bills.

Dear Mr. Cheney,

I did not get the chance to meet you when you came to my farm
a few months back. But knowing the reason for your visit, I thought I
should write in hopes that you remain in contact with Elijah Hall and
Talitha Simms. If this is the case, please pass along to him, or both,
that Solomon passed away on August 27, 1865. He was working in the
cornfields that he loved, and all indications are that his heart gave out on
him. His countenance, however, appeared quite peaceful. Solomon was,
as I'm sure you are aware, one of my former slaves, but I knew him to
be a good and honorable man. My financial circumstances a few years
ago were dire, and it was with great reluctance that I sold his son to help
relieve my debt. After hearing of the brutal treatment inflicted on Elijah,
I have lived with deep regret, and will to my dying day. Please tell Elijah

that his father is buried next to his mama, and that nearly 70 people attended a graveside ceremony performed by Solomon's long-time friend and preacher, Meachum Hungerford.

Sincerely, Josiah Ramsey II

P.S. The cash enclosed is what remains of Solomon's money from the sale of the two horses sold by Harry Warren before he and Elijah departed. Solomon had planned on buying a mule and plow, yet to my knowledge, his only purchase had been a mattress. I hope the money will help give the young couple the start they so deserve.

Oren leaned back in his chair and stared at the empty hearth, longing at once for its mesmerizing flames in which to lose his sorrow. He had developed a kinship, albeit brief, with Solomon, but still it surprised him, the rush of overwhelming sadness he felt for such a grand old man. He shook his head; referring to Solomon as an old man was a misnomer; his oldness was only a reflection of his circumstance. Oren was pleased, at least, to read that Solomon's demise had been recognized by so many friends. His eyes misted when he read that Solomon had purchased a mattress.

He wondered if Albert was scheduled to tutor Elijah in the morning. For a moment he considered going to the Laird farm, but given the hour of the day, he knew it was already too late for the train.

"Fidelia," he called out through his half-opened door. "Do you know if Talitha is on campus this evening?"

"No, Mr. Cheney, she's in Berwick with Elijah. Both will be here in the morning."

Just as well, he pondered. I can deliver the news to them at the same time. "Fidelia, when you see Albert in the morning, please ask him to have Elijah and Talitha meet me in the chapel at ten o'clock."

"Yes, sir. She's always with Elijah so it won't be a problem."

"Thank you."

A light rain fell the next morning as Oren walked to the Freewill Church. Without the sun streaming through its windows, the air inside was cool. He shook the wetness from his hair and hurried to the vestry, where he offered a silent prayer. He sat down on the front pew and waited.

Moments later, the church door opened. Oren stood and watched

Elijah and Talitha, hand in hand, walk down the aisle, a sense of unease on both their faces.

"Something wrong, Mistah Cheney?" asked Elijah.

"I have difficult news for you. Please sit."

Oren waited, and then looked at the two and said, "There's no easy way to tell you. Pappy has died. He has gone home to be in the presence of God."

Talitha leaped from the pew, her hands flying against her chest. Her body rocked on its heels. And then she wailed.

Elijah gritted his teeth, sat in stunned silence, and stared vacantly, yet seeing nothing. At last, his voice halting, he asked, "How he die?"

Oren pulled the envelope from his pocket and held it in his hand. "I received a letter from Josiah Ramsey. Shall I read it to you?"

"Mr. Cheney? Elijah need to read this letter." Reaching for Talitha's hand, he motioned her to sit beside him. Choking back her tears, she pinched her lips closed and sat quietly down.

Oren handed Elijah the envelope and took a step back, his hands clasped behind his back.

Elijah opened the sheet of paper carefully, as if it might otherwise shatter, and saw first the dollar bills in its folds. He took a deep breath, and then began to read out loud.

*"You have seen how a man was made a slave; you shall see
how a slave was made a man."*
—Frederick Douglass

CHAPTER 40
September, 1865

In the days following his father's death, Elijah found his solace in hard, physical labor, comforted by its familiarity and its rhythm. His most poignant memories were that of him and Pappy working side by side in the fields, and in the quiet stillness of dawn, as he made his rounds alone in the barnyard, he remembered and he mourned.

Elijah had also been keenly aware that he was not alone with his grief. In the late mornings, he would break from his chores and with Talitha stroll the pastures and follow the wooded path to the banks along the Little River. And through her eyes, Talitha painted for Elijah a picture of Pappy during the years that he was gone. Her stories, sprinkled with the old man's feistiness, brought sometimes tears and sometimes laughter.

During their quiet mornings together, Elijah had shared with Talitha all the hints of an approaching New England autumn—the green tips of the maple leaves changing to blazing reds and fiery oranges; the flocks of honking geese flying south to their wintering grounds, adventurous squirrels gathering and storing acorns, and the thin layer of morning ice along the edges of the river.

Three weeks later, a letter from Oren Cheney arrived at the Laird household. While he had well understood Elijah's need to step away from the tutoring for a short while, he wanted to pass on the news that Frederick Douglass, travelling on a lecture circuit, would be speaking at Bates College. Oren thought it was an event neither Elijah nor Talitha would want to miss.

That evening at supper, Elijah announced that he wanted to hear Douglass speak, and that he was at last ready to return to his studies.

"Elijah want to hear all what Mistah Douglass say," he said, as Martha ladled bowls of steaming stew from the end of the table.

"Don't give me any of them carrots, Ma," interrupted Jamie.

"You think I haven't heard that before, son?"

Talitha, who had been sitting quietly, unexpectedly began to cry, then just as quickly, held back her tears.

"You don't have to eat them carrots either, Talitha."

"Jamie, mind yourself," snapped Martha.

"You lucky you got carrots to eat," Talitha added.

"Not if you don't like 'em."

"You eat those carrots, child, you hear?" Although Talitha's voice was firm, her tone was lighthearted.

Sheepish, Jamie glanced at Elijah, who shrugged his shoulders and said, "Best do as the missus say."

"I'll have a carrot, Ma. But only one, is all."

Martha winked at Talitha.

"I'm glad to hear you both are returning to Bates," said John as he passed the plate of warm biscuits.

This time Talitha could not hold back her tears.

Martha dropped the ladle in the kettle. "What is it, Talitha?"

"I ain't ready to go back to school, Missus Martha."

"Talk to us, dear."

Elijah reached for Talitha's hand, his eyes glancing around the table.

"I'd like to stay here, if you'll have me. I been cooking and washing, and it all I knows; it feel right. Mr. Cheney, he give me a beautiful room, but I come here to be with Elijah." Talitha could not stop her tears from flowing. Lifting his hand, Elijah gently wiped the wetness from her cheeks.

"It all so new, coming here, and sometimes it just too much. I ain't ready for schoolin'." She took a deep sigh. "There, I go and say it."

"What you need, Talitha, is time," said Martha. "The rest will come. And as far as I'm concerned, you can stay right here." She shot a firm look at her husband.

Leaning back in his chair, and with a hint of a smile, John said, "You'll get no argument from me, my dear."

"Then it's settled," smiled Martha. "As for me, I'm plum delighted for the company."

"What Elijah tell Mistah Cheney?"

"I tell him myself."

"Wish I could tell my teacher that," Jamie grumbled, pushing his carrot under his half-eaten biscuit.

On a gently sloping ridge above the banks of the Androscoggin River, students hurried to their classes at Bates College. Making his own way to Hathorn Hall, Oren smiled as he walked past the bricklayers absorbed in construction of a science building. With a last glance before he entered the hall, he looked out across the grounds and made an instant decision to have the laborers set some trees, and perhaps, he mused, he would plant a garden of flowers in spring. This was to be an eventful day; Frederick Douglass was on campus, and students and faculty were anxious to hear him speak.

Oren was pleased to see Elijah and Talitha arrive at his office. He listened with compassion as Talitha told him she was not yet ready to return to school, not out of grief, but out of a need to feel more settled in her new life. Although disappointed, Oren assured her she would be welcomed back at any time.

From the outer office, Fidelia called, "Mr. Cheney, you've only a few minutes to get Mr. Douglass."

Oren stood and reached for his satchel. "Mr. Douglass was a guest in my home last night and I need to go back and gather him. I'm so glad you came to hear and meet this man. He's a stirring orator."

Frederick Douglass was an imposing figure. Tall, strikingly handsome, his full gray beard could not hide his fine, angular features. He stood behind the pulpit, looked out at the room filled with students and faculty.

"Greetings! It is always a pleasure to be back in New England, my adopted home since the age of twenty, when I escaped on a ship from Baltimore to New Bedford. And it also a pleasure to visit my friend Oren Cheney, whom I first met when he was but a young boy in the home of his parents, Moses and Abigail. Two remarkable people who were staunch abolitionists at a time when there were too few voices that spoke against slavery. I remember his parents promising to pray for me."

Douglass paused and, offering a slight smile, said, *I prayed for twenty years but received no answer until I prayed with my legs."*

Elijah stirred in his seat. "Prayed with my legs! That what Elijah done," he whispered, his mind evoking memories of his race through the forests, Buckra and his dogs close at his heels. Talitha squeezed his hand.

"Oren Cheney continues his parents' legacy of service, and this fine institution is a reflection of the vision and the values of this man. *And I come here today, as I come always to gatherings in New England, preferably as a listener, and not as a speaker, for if anywhere in the country there is to be found the highest sense of justice, or the truest demands for my race, I look for it in the East. I look for it here. The ablest discussions of the whole question of our rights occur here, and to be deprived of the privilege of listening to those discussions is a great deprivation."* He paused, and suddenly the hall filled with applause. Douglass smiled in response.

Elijah stared, reflecting on Douglass's words, "justice" and "I look for it here." Then he cast a hurried glance at Oren, the unending goodness of this man from the East.

"But I also come to you today because our fight is not over. We have won our liberty, but our people are not free unless we have full civil rights. *I am for the immediate, unconditional, and universal enfranchisement of the black man, in every State in the Union. Without this, his liberty is a mockery; without this, you might as well almost retain the old name of slavery for his condition; for in fact, if he is not the slave of the individual master, he is the slave of society, and holds his liberty as a privilege, not as a right."*

Again the room exploded in applause. Elijah felt great stirrings of pride and smiled to himself as he watched Talitha glance about in awe at the white men and women, both young and old, celebrating the words of a colored man.

Douglass expanded for several minutes on the need to press for the black man's right to suffrage, adding that *"The American people are now in tears. The Shenandoah has run blood—the best blood of the North. All around Richmond, the blood of New England and of the North has been shed—of your sons, your brothers and your fathers. We all feel, in the existence of this Rebellion, that judgments terrible, wide-spread, far-reaching, overwhelming, are abroad in the land; and we feel, in view of these judgments, just now, a disposition to learn righteousness. This is the hour. Our streets are in mourning, tears are falling at every fireside, and under the chastisement of this Rebellion we have almost come up to the point of conceding this great, this all-important right of suffrage. I fear that if we fail to do it now, if abolitionists fail to press it now, we may not see, for centuries to come, the same disposition that exists at this moment. Now is time to press this right.*"

Mr. Douglass closed his remarks to a cheering audience. Then, in keeping with his spoken desire to listen, he asked others to speak. Oren led a rousing discussion, and when the formal event came to an end, he asked Douglass to meet briefly with the small group of former slaves. Each had a story to tell, and Douglass, never wavering in attention, reflected, laughed, and sometimes cried with each.

Finally, Douglass turned to Oren. "I'm quite interested in Storer College. I should like to hear more of this new school."

Oren talked for several minutes and then said, "But my commitment with Storer College ends with this fundraising. For the rest of my days, my priority remains here, with Bates College."

"Understandable, my friend. My lecture circuit leads me South soon and I'll plan to visit the school. It sounds as if this will be an institution I could become very much involved with. Perhaps serve on their board."

John Dungy could hardly contain his enthusiasm. "I think what I've heard may have just determined my path following my education. Virginia will always be my home, and with Storer College so close by, I shall seek work there, or at least support it one way or another."

"I wish you great success, John." Turning to the group, Douglass said, "Lastly, to all of you, let me tell you that I believe there are three keys for success in life, and it pleases me more than you know to say that at this moment you all incorporate one of those keys—*to take advantage of every opportunity.* Which you are doing here, obtaining an education. I also implore that you *believe in yourself*—a key that you must hold on to in spite of the challenges, the trials you doubtless will face. And finally, *use the power of the spoken and written word to effect positive change to yourself and to society.* That is what I leave you with."

"Like first person," Elijah whispered to Talitha, who held back her laughter.

As Douglass readied to leave, Elijah and Talitha leaped from their chairs, eager to shake his hand.

"Elijah learn many things from you, Mistah Douglass. Elijah try."

"Of that I have no doubt, young man."

Oren placed a hand on Elijah's shoulder. "The evening I spent with your father? I told Solomon a new day has begun."

Elijah squeezed Talitha's hand. "Yes, suh, Mistah Cheney. A new day."

"Tell me who you love and I will tell you who you are."
—African proverb

CHAPTER 41
October, 1865

"Missus Martha?" Talitha stepped gingerly into the sitting room, a handful of folded linens clutched in her arms. Never had she asked white folk for anything before, and although she was much attached to Martha, she worried her request might still be unbefitting of her place.

She found Martha sitting in the middle of the sofa, flanked on either side by a stack of clothes and a small round box stuffed with a cache of needles and threads. A torn flannel shirt lay across her lap.

"I found these linens in the bottom drawer of the dresser in my room," Talitha said timidly as she held the cloths out for Martha to see.

"Oh, they're nothing but old tablecloths. I don't use them anymore, but I could never bring myself to throw them out."

"If they not used, I means, um," Talitha swallowed, took a deep breath. "You thinks I could have them?"

Looking over her spectacles, Martha furrowed her brow as she fingered through the linens. "They're old and frayed. Whatever will you do with them?"

"Make me a wedding dress."

"Oh, Talitha. I didn't think." Martha let out a long sigh and then in a soft voice she said, "I'm afraid most are stained."

"I knows, but this one," Talitha said, pulling a pale yellow linen from the bottom of her pile and displaying it in her hand, "it got some fine lace on it. Only torn a little, is all. And there are some real nice colors in here, and—"

Hurriedly tucking her needle into the sleeve of the shirt, Martha rose from the sofa and placed her hand gently on Talitha's shoulder. "Come with me, dear."

Confused, a little fearful she would not be given the linens, Talitha hugged them close to her chest as she followed Martha into the bedroom. She watched curiously as Martha lifted open the lid of a large trunk tucked against the end of the spindle bed.

"Been a while since I even looked in here." Martha pulled out a thin blanket and tossed it onto the floor. Then with great care she lifted out a long dress, a pale brown calico patterned with small, delicate flowers a darker shade of brown. A deep, ivory-colored lace trimmed the scooped neckline and finished the long sleeves.

"Do you like it, Talitha?"

"This be one of the prettiest dresses I ever see." She lowered her eyelids, nervously fingering the frayed linens in her arms. "That be your wedding dress?"

Martha nodded. "But I wasn't near as small as you." She laughed. "Maybe with a few tucks, I can give you a proper wedding dress."

"Missus Martha! Oh Lordy! You do that for me?"

"Set those tablecloths on the bed. I want to hold this dress up to you."

Talitha trembled as Martha held the dress against her chest and spread the bodice across her waistline.

"I held on to it thinking if I ever had a daughter, I'd give it to her. But I'll not have you wearing a patchwork of old tablecloths."

When Martha pulled back the dress, Talitha slumped into a chair. "I had me so much anger with Elijah when he go and leave Pappy Sol and me. I so hurt, I almost take up with someone I didn't love. But Mr. Cheney, he come down and tell me Elijah love me still. I was so afeared of stepping into the white folks' world, and now you go and give me your wedding dress. Missus Martha, my eyes is opening wide, like my Elijah's done long time ago. This everything to me. And I ain't never forget your kindness."

"That first night together, when you said you wanted to follow after Jamie, to be the one to talk to my son instead of Elijah, I had a feeling you'd say all the right things to him. I'm not sure any of us knew how to handle Jamie anymore—his grief, his attachment to Elijah so strong he couldn't let go. His emotions owned us all, so afraid we were of his slipping inside himself again. But you handled him."

Martha drew a long breath and continued, "You gave me my son back. This is a way to thank you." Suddenly she laughed once again. "I think those tablecloths might have a use after all! You're going to need a crinoline."

The autumn winds howled across the meadowlands, stripping the last of the dying leaves from the aged oaks and gray sugar maples that rimmed Cranberry Meadow Road to the Laird farm. Inside, a fire blazed in the hearth, and a small gathering of wedding guests mingled quietly, unmindful of the windy, cold October eve.

Elijah stood to one side of the hearth, handsome in his new trousers and white shirt. He fidgeted nervously with the cravat around his neck and glanced over at Harry, who flashed him a knowing smile. A month earlier, Harry had at last married his childhood sweetheart in a beautiful church wedding. Across from Elijah, Oren stood silently, a Bible clasped in his hands.

Martha slipped off her white apron and with her hands smoothed the folds of her pale blue gingham, tugging gently at its soft lace bodice. She blushed when she looked up and saw her husband across the room studying her. She tapped Jamie on the shoulder, pushed a hank of still damp hair from his face, and nudged him toward the hearth. Flushed with importance as Elijah's best man, Jamie hurried to stand beside him.

The guests moved into place. John Dungy stood just steps away from Oren. He could not help but grin at the image before him—Jamie curled in the folds of Elijah's arms. John had become a good friend to Elijah and Talitha, and not long after their first meeting in Oren's office, he had sat with Elijah and penned a letter to William Still.

Harry and his wife, Mary, moved closer to the hearth; Leonard and Mabel Tasker and Clay Ricker stood beside them. Excusing herself, Elizabeth Ricker reached for her violin on a small pine table and hurried to the back of the room. Reverend Snow walked over to stand beside John Laird behind the others.

"It's good to see you smile easily again, John," said Reverend Snow quietly, his thinning hair disheveled from the wind.

"Been a long couple of years, Reverend."

"God closed a door, make no mistake. But he opened a window. You've a fine family here."

"There is that. I feel some joy at last."

The silvery timbre of the violin lifted through the room.

Martha opened the bedroom door.

Talitha stepped into view, her pale brown calico flowing to the floor. Her coppery-colored hair fell in ringlets around her long, lovely face, and her round eyes danced like rays of sunlight as she moved gracefully to the hearth.

Slipping from Elijah's embrace, Jamie smiled at Talitha as she came to stand beside Elijah.

Oren began. "Elijah and Talitha, divine revelation has declared marriage to be honorable in all." He spoke for several minutes and then said, "Will the parties now join hands for the exchange of vows."

Turning first to Elijah, Oren asked, "Do you, Elijah Hall, take Talitha Simms, whom you now hold by hand, as your true and lawful wife; and God helping you, will you love and cherish, honor and protect her, cleaving only and ever unto her, until God by death shall separate you?"

"Elijah do—No! Not Elijah!"

Talitha gasped.

Elijah stole a hurried glance at Oren and then turned his face back to Talitha. "I do. Not Elijah do. I do."

Oren suppressed a smile, and remembering once again the fugitive slave he'd met in childhood, to himself he said, "Luther, if you are looking down on me, know that we have prospered here at last."

Oren led Talitha through her vow.

Finally, Oren said, "It is the duty of both to delight each in the society of the other; to preserve an inviolable fidelity, and to see to it that what God has thus joined together, man never puts asunder." Unexpectedly, Oren turned and whispered to John Dungy, who nodded and quickly disappeared into the kitchen.

Faces locked in curiosity when the tall colored man returned carrying two brooms.

"Elijah," Oren said, "I must confess that Talitha and John, without your knowledge, asked that we close this ceremony with a thread from the past. Guests, what follows is an old ritual often used in the weddings of slaves. It's called 'jumping the broom.' Many farm slaves, without the benefit of clergy, used instead this tradition to signify marriage."

Oren continued, "Elijah, this is Talitha's gift to you. Your father once told her the story of how he and your mother were married in this way."

Elijah turned to Talitha, his heart beating rapidly against his chest.

"John, please set the brooms."

John Dungy placed a broom at Talitha and Elijah's feet.

"I now ask the couple to each step across the brooms at the same time while their hands are joined."

Elijah and Talitha smiled at one another. Joined hands.

And jumped over the brooms.

Oren said, "You both are now truly married."

Everyone clapped.

Raising his hand, Oren said, "Another moment, please. I understand that there is another part to this tradition. Talitha tells me that on the farms, each partner was required to also jump backward over a broom that is held a foot above the ground. If one partner fails to clear the broom, the other partner is declared the one who would rule or "boss" the household. If both partners clear the broom without touching it, it's my understanding there would be no bossing from a single partner."

Thanking John Dungy, Oren then asked Harry to come forward and stand with Jamie. "Harry, please hold and raise the broom a foot above the floor in front of Elijah. And Jamie, please do the same for Talitha."

Jamie started giggling. "I already know who the boss is."

Laughter erupted. Even Talitha could not hold back her smile.

Jamie raised the broom as high as Talitha's waist.

"Lower that broom, child."

"Elijah and Talitha, turn your backs to the brooms."

Talitha hiked up the folds of her dress. When the couple was ready, Oren said, "You may jump."

Both cleared the brooms without touching.

"Lost your only chance, Elijah," whispered Jamie.

The violin sang out and even the wind rapping a beat against the window panes seemed in step with the clapping hands and dancing feet in joyous celebration.

"When a man starts out with nothing,
When a man starts out with his hands
Empty, but clean,
When a man starts to build a world,
He starts first with himself
And the faith that is in his heart—
The strength there,
The will there to build."
—Langston Hughes, *Freedom's Plow,*
first published in *Opportunity, 1943*

CHAPTER 42
August, 1866

It was the first time corn had been planted on the Laird farm, and Elijah strolled among the healthy green stalks now inching higher than his shoulders. He paused, carefully spread open a silky tuft, looked at the yellowing kernels and smiled, pleased that the corn would be ready for picking by the end of the week. Mistah John had given him five acres to build a home for him and Talitha, and instantly Elijah knew he wanted to take one acre and plant corn. Harry had offered to help, and in exchange, Elijah offered him half the crop's yield. He smiled at the memory of that bright June morning when, with Harry, his wife, Mary, Jamie, and Talitha, he had hoed the freshly plowed earth and planted the corn seeds. Talitha had grown very fond of Mary, and not long after attending the lecture with Frederick Douglass in the autumn, she had asked Mary to teach her to read. And through the long winter Talitha had begun to believe in herself.

Elijah stepped away from the row of stalks, moved up the hill and sat down on the warm ground, his elbows resting on his knees. The acre was, in part, his tribute to Pappy, and as the breeze blew soft around him, he tapped a fisted hand against his heart. "Right there, Pappy, you living right there." But planting the corn was also a means to reconcile one of his own more haunting memories.

The last time he had been in a cornfield, he had crawled on his hands and knees, fearful of being seen by slave catchers or farmers who could capture him and return him to his master. Running for weeks, with no food except a chance berry patch, he had been in desperate need of nourishment. So starved was he that he had risked crawling among the broken, withered corn stalks, all the while knowing their harvest had been long since picked. Still he had scavenged the ground, praying he might find abandoned ears carelessly dropped by a field hand in haste to fill his sack. He had found only a single ear and even though its kernels were dry, bleached by the sun, he had gnawed at them like a wild boar.

He shook his head, picked a blade of tall grass and chewed its end. How was it possible to have come this far, to sit peacefully on a hillside, to plant and reap the yield of his own cornfield? Again, he tapped his fisted hand against his heart. "I know how this came to be, where this all begin—with you, Billy, suh." Their unlikely paths had crossed ever so briefly, yet for Elijah it had been a fated connection that had secured for him a future.

His nightmares occurred less frequently now that Buckra was no longer an ever-constant threat. For two years it was always Jamie who had raced into his room and wakened him from his nightmares, rescuing him from the demons of his past. Then Jamie would climb into his bed and curl against his back in sleep. Now his beautiful Talitha slept peacefully by his side.

"Jamie, suh," he mused. The grief that had owned his young soul for so long had finally released its grip. Elijah was glad he had been able to keep his promise to camp with Jamie in the woods, the child's once-secret hideaway where he had hoped to hide his brother from the army. They had fished the Little River and cooked their trout over a fire in the same way he and Billy had at Goose Creek. He also discovered that playing out this simple act had seemingly been a last hurdle; Jamie was ready to leave his grief and his childhood behind.

The sound of footsteps running through the grass brought him back to the moment. He blinked at the blinding sun and shielded his eyes as he raised his face.

"I found you." Jamie plopped down beside him, licorice strings bulging in his shirt pocket.

"You been to Blaisdell's Store again, Jamie, suh?"

"Yeah."

"Emma there? She go and give them to you?"

"Nope. Bought 'em myself."

"Mmm-hmm."

Suddenly Jamie jumped to his feet. "Here they come!"

With the sun at her back, Talitha made her way around the rows of corn and up the hill, a small blue bundle cradled in her arms.

Elijah smiled. Although Talitha had grown very fond of Jamie, she steadfastly refused to coddle him. Unabashed, Jamie shadowed her like a dutiful child.

Talitha lowered herself to the ground. A soft cooing lifted from the blanket.

"Can I hold him, Talitha?"

"Yes, child, but sit yourself back down." She waited as Jamie plopped down again and then gently placed the infant in his arms. "Careful now—keep a hand under his head," she directed. "He barely a few days old and he can't hold hisself up."

Jamie peered at the tiny brown face. "I think he went back to sleep."

Elijah leaned over and with his finger lightly stroked the infant's fuzzy head. "He sleeping all right."

"He's awful little."

With the August sun bearing down, Talitha lifted the blanket over the infant's face. "He grow fast, child."

"Wonder what he'll be when he grows up," Jamie asked.

"I think he be whatever he want," said Elijah. "Whatever he want."

Tiny feet wiggled out from under the blanket. Grinning, Elijah gently stroked each toe. "But he got himself some mighty big shoes to fill."

He folded the blanket over the baby's feet. "You hear what your Pappy say, Billy Solomon?"

AFTERWORD

M any readers of *Billy Boy, The Sunday Soldier of the 17th Maine* asked me to continue with Elijah's story. While the idea intrigued me, I wanted to create a plausible story within a Maine historical context. A friend of mine, Bill Hierstein, told me that Bates College recruited a small number of former slaves after the Civil War and suggested I further research its history. To my great delight, I found a story worth telling in the founder of Bates College, Oren Cheney, one of the most fascinating figures in Maine's history. An examination of Cheney's public life reveals he is associated most visibly as the founder and first president of Bates College, which evolved from its first charter as the Maine State Seminary in 1857. I chose to shed light on a perhaps lesser-known facet of this man's character: his steadfast commitment to the abolition of slavery, including his efforts to help secure access to education for emancipated slaves. Elijah's story parallels this theme.

With the exception of Cheney's fictitious friendship with Elijah, the glimpses I reveal of this man throughout the novel are based on fact and were drawn in large part from *The Story of the Life and Work of Oren B. Cheney,* written by his wife Emeline, who drew much of her work from Cheney's diaries. When italicized, dialogue attributed to Cheney is factual; the sources used came from the Edmund S. Muskie Archives and Special Collections Library, Bates College, Lewiston, Maine.

A Freewill Baptist, Oren Cheney was strongly influenced by his parents, Moses and Abigail, whose home in Peterborough, New Hampshire, was, in fact, a station on the Underground Railroad. Notables such as Frederick Douglass and Harriet Tubman were guests in his parents' home.

In 1843, at the age of twenty-seven, Oren Cheney became principal and preacher at Parsonsfield Academy in Maine. When he had accepted the ministry at the Fourth Free Will Baptist church in Lebanon in

1846, he not only felt the full responsibilities of pastoral care to an entire community, but also believed that education should be a strong component of that commitment. On the corner of the parsonage lot in Lebanon stood a little red schoolhouse, and shortly after his arrival, Oren became its teacher, eager to imbue its students with a desire to learn. A year later, one of the community's prominent citizens, David Cowell, offered Oren a lot of land and a hundred dollars to build an academy. Oren had immediately seen his offer as "an invitation and a challenge," and raised an additional $1,000 for its construction. Lebanon Academy opened its doors in 1847.

Parsonsfield Seminary's burning to the ground in 1854 brought to the surface Oren's long held concern about the numbers of young people scattered throughout Maine's villages and farms without the means of obtaining a good education. He imagined founding a new school, not merely a replacement of the beloved Parsonsfield Seminary, but a different school, "a high order or grade somewhere between a College and an Academy, in a more centrally located part of the state." Three years later, the Maine State Seminary in Lewiston, chartered by the Maine Legislature, opened its doors. The story of how the Maine State Seminary evolved to Bates College is compelling, and I urge any interested reader to read *Bates College and its Background* by Alfred Williams Anthony.

Unfortunately, most of Oren Cheney's diaries are lost to history. I gleaned specific passages found in Emeline's book. For example, Oren diverts from his business trip in Washington to Richmond in the final days of the war. In his diary he states, "visited and talked hopefully with the Confederate prisoners." With the insight of Pastor Trent Boyd, we developed what we believe to be a realistic visit with the prisoners and the message that Oren Cheney would have wanted to convey. The discovery and distribution of the small Testaments from the American Bible Association was factual, including the prisoners on the third floor who lowered bags on strings in order to obtain additional Testaments.

And, true to Bill Hierstein's words, Oren Cheney did, in fact, seek out a handful of former slaves in Virginia after the Civil War to attend Bates College. Although his greatest priority was Bates, one of Oren Cheney's most intriguing accomplishments was raising $10,000 in matching funds for Storer College in Harper's Ferry, West Virginia, an institution to educate and train former slaves. Freewill Baptists throughout New

England played a significant role in establishing schools in the South for freed slaves, and Reverend Nathan Brackett founded what later became Storer College. John Storer, a generous philanthropist from Sanford, Maine, made the initial matching gift and clearly deserved mention in my novel.

The story of the Confederate soldier buried in Gray, Maine is factual.

Salisbury Prison in North Carolina is factual, including Sarah Johnson and her poignant acts to help the wounded, and burying the body of Hugh Berry, a Union soldier under her care, in her garden.

I excerpted parts of President Lincoln's speech to the emancipated slaves when he walked the streets of Richmond in April, 1865, with his son Tad.

I took liberties with the timelines of two key events. While the school in Harper's Ferry began shortly after the Civil War, Congress only officially approved the lots of land and buildings for Storer College in 1868. Oren Cheney played a key role in amending the original legislation to include larger lots of land for the college. Also, Frederick Douglass did visit Bates College, but it was a few years after the war. I used excerpts of his speech "What the Black Man Wants" that was delivered at the annual meeting of the Massachusetts Anti-Slavery Society in April 1865; this was the message he lectured tirelessly about in the post-war years. I also incorporated Douglass's three keys to success in life, which he spoke to often: believe in yourself, take advantage of every opportunity, and use the power of the spoken and written language to effect positive change for yourself and society.

Former slaves Alexander Sanders, Hamilton Keyes, and John Dungy attended Bates College. Of great interest to Trent and me was that, as the research unfolded, we saw that Elijah's story in large part mirrored the real account of John Dungy, who escaped slavery, met with William Still and the Vigilance Committee in Philadelphia, arrived in Canada, and later returned as a free man and attended Bates College.

In closing, the Reverend Thomas Hobbs Stacy, in *The Morning Star,* July 14, 1898, says of Oren Cheney, "It is a matter of just pride when one has passed through an eventful public life with no stain upon the character, no mark of dishonesty, no act unworthy a Christian."

Look for these other great books by Jean M. Flahive

Billy Boy, The Sunday Soldier of the 17th Maine

Remember Me, Tomah Joseph's Gift to Franklin Roosevelt

The Galloping Horses of Willowbrook